Praise for Elle Kennedy's *Dance of Seduction*

"Dance of Seduction is a wonderful love story... With two wonderful romances that tug at the heart strings, I recommend Elle Kennedy's Dance of Seduction."

~ *Katie, Fallen Angels Reviews*

Look for these titles by
Elle Kennedy

Now Available:

Bad Moon Rising
Heat of the Moment
Going For It
Midnight Encounters

Print Anthologies
Midsummer Night's Steam: Hot Summer Nights

Dance of Seduction

Elle Kennedy

A Samhain Publishing, Ltd. publication.

Samhain Publishing, Ltd.
577 Mulberry Street, Suite 1520
Macon, GA 31201
www.samhainpublishing.com

Dance of Seduction
Copyright © 2009 by Elle Kennedy
Print ISBN: 978-1-60504-089-9
Digital ISBN: 1-59998-902-6

Editing by Laurie Rauch
Cover by Scott Carpenter

First Samhain Publishing, Ltd. electronic publication: March 2008
First Samhain Publishing, Ltd. print publication: January 2009

Dedication

To my critique partners for being so darn supportive, and to my editor for letting me know how she feels about wandering body parts...

Chapter One

Find her and bring her home.

Luke Russell repeated the words in his head, over and over again, as he glanced around the dim-lit club. Well, club was an exaggeration. The Dancehall was nothing more than a bar with a stage in the corner. But hey, if calling it a club made the owner feel better, more power to him.

"Another beer?"

Luke looked down at the longneck he'd been nursing, and then up at the redheaded waitress. "No, thanks. I'm good. When is the show going to start?"

The woman shrugged and her ample breasts, barely contained by her low-cut belly top, bobbed in front of his face. "A few minutes. The dancers are just warming up."

He stared at the drawn velvet curtains shielding the small stage area. Was Ellie behind those curtains?

He wanted to ask the waitress what kind of show this was. A part of him prayed it was a ballet. God, how he prayed. But that seemed far-fetched, considering the atmosphere. Most of the patrons littering the bar's tables were male, though he did spot a few females. Everyone wore shorts, T-shirts, sandals— hardly the kind of attire one associated with tutus and classical music. Yet, despite the casual environment, Luke continued to maintain some degree of hope that at any second the curtain would open to reveal dancers in elegant leotards and the bar would fill with the tasteful sound of Tchaikovsky.

Glancing back at the waitress, he tried to hold on to that hope. "By any chance, does the show feature ballet dancers?"

Her blue eyes grew wary. "Ballet? Honey, I think you're in the wrong place."

"Waitress!"

"Excuse me," she said before flouncing off in the direction of the heavy-set man who'd just signaled her.

He watched her go, all hope deflating in his chest. Well, how bad could it really be? He directed his gaze to the stage area, deciding the place looked fairly tame. A piano sat in the corner of the room, the man on the bench smoking a cigar, looking bored. Everyone else in the bar was engaged in idle chatter and the occasional burst of laugher rang out.

He sipped his beer, suddenly wishing he were back in San Francisco. The temperature down here in San Valdez was grueling, far hotter than he'd expected, and his black T-shirt seemed to attract the heat, even indoors. But hell, it beat the expensive suits he'd been forced to wear just a couple months ago. Not to mention those stuffy tuxedos. Guarding a senator didn't provide one with the luxury of jeans, and he knew he should be grateful for the reprieve.

Unfortunately, comfortable attire didn't exactly make his current situation any less annoying. Sometimes he wished he'd never heard of the word *loyalty*. Those who knew him said his loyal nature was his best quality, and it did come in handy in his line of work. This time, however, he wondered if he should've put his foot down and told Josh Dawson to find someone else for the job.

Bottom line: Josh wanted his sister to come home. And since he didn't trust anyone else to do it, he'd asked his best friend to make it happen. Easier said than done, of course. Luke had no clue why Ellie Dawson had decided to run off to this obscure one-horse town but he was fairly certain she wouldn't leave without a fight. There would be no white flag with Ellie, no calm surrender, no complacent obedience.

She was going to give him hell—fire and brimstone included.

"Ladies and gentlemen..."

Luke lifted his head as a male voice blared over the loudspeaker and the lights in the bar dimmed. A spotlight focused on the stage as the voice continued. "Get ready to go wild!"

Go wild?

"You all know 'em. You all love 'em. Give a big hand for...the Dancehall Dolls!"

Before Luke could register that odd introduction, the curtains parted.

Dear Lord, Ellie, what are you doing?

A sexy jazz tune filled the bar as the half-dozen figures on the stage began to move. The dancers were not wearing the tutus and ballet slippers Luke had hoped to see. Not wearing much at all, in fact. He saw lace and mesh, some sequins, and a lot of skin. Too much skin.

Danger! his head shouted. His traitorous eyes, however, refused to unglue from the sight in front of him.

The dancers moved in sync, everything choreographed, from their high kicks to the way they spun around and wiggled their hips. One by one, each girl made her way to the front of the stage for a sultry solo.

It wasn't until the third dancer came up that Luke nearly choked on his beer.

Elenore Dawson.

He could've picked her out of a line-up, having known her for more than half his life, yet the sexy temptress up on that stage looked nothing like the girl he'd watched grow up.

She wore a tight black corset, a strap of black mesh that constituted a skirt, and a pair of stilettos that made her appear far taller than her five feet, four inches. Long brown hair cascaded down her shoulders in waves, and her blue eyes looked huge with all that smoky eyeliner surrounding them.

Luke's mouth went bone-dry. Oh, man, Josh was going to kill him. Josh was going to kill *her*. How had a ballerina ended up performing a mind-blowing jazz dance in a tiny town on the Mexican border?

And why did her breasts look so damn good? They couldn't be that big. He remembered them being small, perky. Had to be the corset. And those stilettos did amazing things to her legs.

She whirled around, and the sight of her firm, round behind shaking on that stage made his groin tighten.

This couldn't be Ellie Dawson. His P.I. friend had obviously made a mistake.

It had to be a mistake.

He watched the rest of the show, which lasted too long for his frantic brain and aroused body. It couldn't be her. Ellie simply wasn't this...sexy.

On the stage, the dancers took a few bows as the music came to an end. The second the overhead lights flickered on and the curtains closed, Luke shot to his feet.

He needed to look at that dark-haired vixen with his own two eyes and make sure she wasn't the woman he was searching for.

Make sure she wasn't his best friend's kid sister.

"Great moves," Vivian Kendrick said, approaching Ellie's vanity area.

Ellie saw her boss's reflection in the mirror and smiled. "Thanks, Viv. I improvised there in the end."

"Well, whatever you did worked. I had about six customers come up to me and ask about you."

Ellie reached for a cotton ball and began removing the heavy makeup from her face. God, if people only knew how much time went into getting ready for a show. And how much time it took returning to normal afterwards.

"One is actually waiting outside the door. Said he wants to come in and get an autograph," Vivian added.

She wrinkled her nose. An autograph? She'd been dancing here in Vivian's club for nearly two months now, and this was the first time someone had wanted an autograph. "Who is it?" she asked.

Vivian shrugged. "Just a customer. But he's cute. Real cute. Should I send him in?"

She tossed the cotton ball in the wastebasket and reached for another one. "Sure, no harm in that, I guess. Just stay close by."

"I always do."

Vivian left the dressing room, and Ellie continued to wipe the makeup from her face. God, she hated makeup. Hated these skimpy little outfits too. It was funny how, in ballet, she wore just as little clothing, yet something about her tutus and leotards seemed elegant. Sophisticated.

She glanced down at the corset and tiny skirt. Nope, not sophisticated. More like trashy.

The dressing room had emptied out, and as usual, she was

13

the last one there. All the other dancers didn't bother scrubbing off their layers of makeup. Most of the girls wore that stuff on a daily basis, not just for the shows. She liked having the room to herself, though. It reminded her of all the times she'd gotten ready alone for her ballet recitals.

As she got rid of the last of her eye shadow, she heard the sound of the door opening. Right, her fan. Stifling a sigh, she swiveled the chair and turned to face her admirer.

She gasped.

"Oh, damn it to hell. It *is* you."

Luke Russell strode into the dressing room, slamming the door behind him.

All Ellie could do was gape. What was he doing here? And how had he found her? She hadn't thought anyone would think to track her down in San Valdez. Heck, if it weren't for Vivian, Ellie wouldn't even know about the place herself. North of Tijuana and right on the Pacific coastline, the beach town was so remote it wasn't even listed on most maps. And, she'd thought, the last place anyone would think to look for her.

But Luke had found her.

Because of Josh.

Of course. There was no other reason why Luke Russell would be here. Her older brother must have enlisted the help of his best friend to find her.

The thought sent a jolt of anger to her gut. Why couldn't Josh respect her wishes? Before she'd left San Francisco, she'd made it clear she needed time and space. And what had he done? Not even two months had passed and he'd gone out and sent his henchman to track her down.

"What are you doing here?" she said, though she was fairly certain of the answer. She tried to keep her tone calm, even, but inside she was fuming over her brother's insensitivity.

"I think the question is what are *you* doing here?" His voice was rough.

Oh, no, she'd completely forgotten about his voice. His entirely sexy voice. She'd also forgotten how good-looking he was.

Luke took a step toward her chair, his smoky gray eyes flickering with anger and disbelief. His dark brown hair was a little longer, falling onto his forehead in a way it hadn't the last time she'd seen him. When had that been?

Bitterness tugged at her throat. Right, two years ago. At her and Scott's engagement party. He'd been in the middle of an assignment, but he'd made a brief appearance. Stopped by before any of the guests arrived, wished her and Scottie well, and then disappeared. She hadn't seen or heard from him since, which meant he really had no right storming into her life like this and making demands.

"Are you going to answer the question?" he demanded, standing in front of her with his hands on his lean hips.

"Are you going to answer mine?" she shot back.

Luke's body stiffened in a sexy way that made his wide chest contract against the snug black T-shirt he wore. He was still as broad and powerful as ever, a fact that didn't escape her. She'd fantasized about that hard body many times during her teenage years.

"Why are you dressed up like that? Why the hell are you in this damn town? Why are you strutting around half-naked on the stage of a second-rate club?" His questions fired out like bullets from a rifle.

She resisted the urge to roll her eyes. She'd also forgotten how commanding—and demanding—this man could be. "I'm not answering anything until you tell me why you're here."

15

His eyes darkened. "I'm here to take you home."

"Forget it."

Rising from the chair, she walked to the other side of the room, where she grabbed her robe from one of the hooks on the wall. She wouldn't talk to him while wearing this skimpy outfit. She wouldn't give him the upper hand.

She slipped on the robe and tightened the sash, then turned to glance at Luke. He looked furious.

"This isn't the time to be stubborn, Elenore. Get dressed. We're going back to San Francisco."

"No, we're not, *Lucas.*"

She didn't appreciate him talking to her like an insolent child. He'd always treated her like a kid, since the day she'd met him. And sure, she was only twenty-four, six years younger than Luke, but that didn't give him the right to order her around.

"Seriously, Ellie, you won't win. I'm not leaving this goddamned town until you pack up your things and come home with me."

"Then I guess you'll be staying around for a long time, won't you?" She used the sweetest voice she could muster.

He let out a growl and she almost grinned at the sheer exasperation in his eyes. Riling him up had always been one of her favorite pastimes. She'd had such a crush on him when she was younger, and since he'd never paid a single morsel of attention to her, the only way she'd gotten him to notice her was by irritating him. As the years passed, she hadn't been able to kick the habit of getting under Luke's skin. Making him crazy. Not so much for the power trip it provided but for the satisfaction she got knowing she affected him.

"So," she continued, strolling back to the vanity and

reaching for a hairbrush, "you can tell my brother he's wasted everyone's time by sending you here."

Luke didn't answer.

"What, you think I don't know Joshua is behind this?" She ran the brush through her long hair and arched a taunting brow in Luke's direction.

"He's just worried about you," Luke finally said, his husky voice quiet.

Her hand faltered for a moment, nearly dropping the hairbrush, but she tried to regain her composure. She knew Josh was worried about her, had been ever since the car accident that had put a screeching halt to her ballet career. And after Scott had broken off their engagement, Josh's worry only increased.

Rather than being supportive and patient, however, he'd kept pushing her to get over it. Like she ever could. Josh didn't know the whole story, but the parts he did should've made him realize she wasn't ready to forget. In one split-second her entire world had crashed down around her, and her brother wanted her to pretend it never happened?

She'd grown so tired of Josh's pressure, so tired of waking up every morning knowing the grim reality of her future. So she'd left. Packed up her bags and moved to a place where no one knew her, where no one had any expectations of her, where there were no reminders of what she'd lost.

She should've known her peaceful existence would be disturbed.

"He doesn't need to worry about me." She set down the hairbrush and reached for an elastic band, then tied her hair up in a loose ponytail.

"Really?" Luke raised one dark brow. "After what I just saw, I'd say Josh has plenty to worry about. How could you put

17

yourself on display like that?"

Her lips tightened. "I was just dancing."

"Dancing? You call shaking your ass dancing? You call flashing your tits in the faces of drunken men dancing?"

Fury began pumping through her blood. "Excuse me? I did no such thing!"

The furious sparks in Luke's eyes matched the ones sizzling in her body. He took a step closer, and she gasped as he tore open her robe and exposed her flimsy costume.

"Look at what you're wearing," he said, his voice low, menacing.

She swallowed as his gaze roamed over her body, as those gray eyes focused on her chest and the cleavage spilling over the corset. Then his gaze lowered to her legs and she swallowed harder. Everywhere he looked, she burned. Hot flames licked at her skin, and her knees began to wobble.

Get it together!

Right. She wouldn't give him the upper hand. She wouldn't let a silly old crush make her back down.

"You can't tell me you don't like what I'm wearing." Her tone challenging, she arched her back, knowing very well her chest jutted out as she did so.

He glanced at her breasts, and his Adam's apple bobbed as he gulped. "I hate what you're wearing," he muttered.

She moved her barely-clad body inches from his. "You're saying you don't like seeing a woman in a skimpy outfit?" She twisted her mouth in a smirk. "From what Josh told me, you like your women with as little clothing as possible. So what's the problem?"

Luke's mouth set in a tight line. "The problem is my best friend's kid sister is dancing practically naked in front of strangers."

Kid sister.

Of course. That was all she'd ever be to him, wasn't it?

She took a step back and closed her robe. "I'm old enough to make my own decisions. And if I choose to dance practically naked in front of strangers, I damn well can." She scowled. "You can take that message back to my brother."

"I already told you, I'm not leaving without you."

"And I already told you, I'm not going anywhere."

Their eyes locked, and she refused to back down. She knew Luke was a stubborn man—annoyingly so—but she was just as stubborn. And she wasn't going to allow him to force her into anything.

"Ellie." He sighed. "Don't be difficult."

"I was born difficult."

She saw his mouth twitch, as if he wanted to laugh, but she knew he wouldn't. Luke was the king of cool, always had been.

"You're really starting to piss me off, Ellie."

"What else is new?" She paused. "You might as well go now. You're just wasting your time. I'm not leaving."

"Fine."

She lifted her eyebrows. "Fine what?" Suspicion tugged at her stomach. Luke Russell didn't give up this easily. He never gave up, actually.

"Stay," he said lightly.

"Really?" She couldn't help but wonder if maybe this time he would let it go. Maybe this time he would stop being so pigheaded and let her live her own life.

"Sure. Stay." He shot her a lazy grin. "Should we have

dinner tonight, or tomorrow? The sign outside says the first show finishes at eight and the next one doesn't start 'til ten, so we have time if you want to go now."

"Huh?"

"Tomorrow, then."

"Aren't you going to leave?"

His grin widened. "Nope."

Of course it wouldn't be this easy.

"Luke, be logical. You have a job, a life. Maybe even a girlfriend—" she snorted, "—although I can't picture that one. You can't stay here."

"Why not? I'm between assignments right now."

She tried to keep the desperation at bay. "You won't convince me to go back."

"Like I said, as long as you're here, I'm here. Deal with it."

He looked so positively smug that she wanted to throw something at him. Why couldn't he and her brother just leave her alone? Why couldn't they let her lick her wounds in peace?

"Go home, Lucas." Her voice came out as a whisper.

He held her gaze, smug, satisfied, stubborn. "Not until you do, Elenore. Not until you do."

Chapter Two

The next evening, Luke finally worked up the nerve to call Ellie's brother. The call went exactly as he'd expected.

"She's doing what?"

Luke held the cell phone away from his ear, afraid if Josh yelled any louder, his eardrums would burst. He hadn't expected the guy to be pleased with the news, but there was no need to roar.

"Why didn't you drag her off that stage?" Josh sounded livid.

Luke grinned to himself. "Drag her? She would've ripped my eyes out."

"Better you blind than Ellie stripping in front of strangers."

"She wasn't stripping. She was dancing. Just not ballet."

"Listen to me, man, you need to bring her home right now."

"I'm working on it," Luke said in a calm voice.

He raked his fingers through his dark hair and stared up at the neon sign blinking over the front doors of the club. Damn, he didn't look forward to going back in there. Seeing Ellie in that skimpy costume again.

"I'm going crazy with worry here, Luke."

What else was new? Josh had been worrying about his sister for as long as Luke could remember. He'd met Josh in sophomore year at high school, the year after Josh and Ellie's parents had died in a boating accident. The Dawson siblings had been living with an aunt in San Francisco, though the woman was hardly what you'd call a responsible guardian. She was rarely home for her niece and nephew and, as a result, Josh became both father and mother to nine-year-old Ellie.

Over the years, Luke watched as Josh's protective nature became almost stifling. He could be enormously unreasonable when it came to Ellie, but this time, Luke agreed with his friend's position—Ellie didn't belong in a corset and stilettos, dancing for a few beach locals. She belonged at home.

"Don't worry. I know what I'm doing. Protecting people is what I do, remember?"

"Just take care of her. Don't let her coax you into leaving without her. I want my little sister home. No more of this nonsense."

After he hung up the phone, Luke stared once again at the flashing sign. Under it was a small advertisement for the Dancehall Dolls, who apparently were quite popular among the townsfolk. Well, no kidding. Sexy women dancing to sexy jazz tunes? Why wouldn't they be popular?

He blew out a breath. What had possessed her to move out to the middle of nowhere and become a dancing *doll*? Why hadn't she returned to the Hartford Ballet Company?

He'd never understand Ellie. She was a complete mystery to him, always had been. And she'd always managed to drive him mad. As a kid, she'd been his shadow, following his teenage self around everywhere, annoying him with her pesky questions. As a college coed, whenever he and Josh had gone to visit her, she would purposely try to make him angry with her sarcasm and sheer stubbornness. Even now, when he hadn't seen her in two years, she got to him.

Why was she here? He couldn't even begin to figure it out. He knew about the car accident, how she'd broken her foot and had to take a break from ballet. But her foot was healed now—she'd proven at the club that she could move around on it. The company she toured with was one of the most prestigious in the country. Why had she given it up to become a Dancehall Doll?

He shoved the cell phone in his back pocket and took another breath, knowing all his questions would go unanswered the longer he loitered out here. The sound of music wafted from the open doors and he prayed it was just a song from the jukebox. The first show was supposed to be over by now. God, did he hope it was over. Because he couldn't see Ellie in that corset again.

He didn't think his dick could handle it.

Ω

Josh Dawson slammed down the telephone and let out a string of curses that had his secretary gasping. He was a little surprised to lift his head and find Alice lurking in the doorway since normally he knew where all his staff was at any given moment. He wasn't going to apologize for his foul mood, though. After three years as his secretary, Alice was probably used to his temper.

"What is it?" he grumbled, leaning back in his leather chair.

"I finished making those phone calls." Her expression was meek and timid, a common look among the people who worked for him.

Josh had once overheard one of his paralegals comment he was wound so tight that "one day the guy will explode," an outcome that wasn't far from unlikely. At fourteen, Josh's entire life had changed. He'd had to grow up fast, and with growing up came a load of responsibilities, the main one being his little sister. After their parents died, he'd become her protector. He'd fast-tracked through high school, gone to law school, found himself a stable, well-paying career, all for Ellie's sake. His goal had been to keep her safe, secure and happy, and he thought he'd done a good job.

Until she'd decided to take off, of course.

"Boss?"

Josh lifted his head. "Sorry, what were you saying, Alice?"

"I called those places in San Valdez, like you asked."

"And?"

She held out a few sheets of paper. "All the information is here. Your sister rented a bungalow, paid in full for one year. I also checked out some of the other residents, and the only one who could be useful is Kendrick."

A sharp look instantly creased his features. "Kendrick?"

Alice glanced down at her notes. "Yeah, a Vivian Kendrick. On the list you gave me there was a Tanya Kendrick, your sister's old roommate. Maybe they're related."

"They are," Josh muttered to himself. With a dismissive wave of his hand, he added, "Thanks, Alice. Leave the info here and start heading home, okay?"

With a nod, Alice took a few steps forward, dropped the papers on his desk and turned for the door. The second the petite blonde left the office he let out a long breath. Vivian. So that's where she'd gone. Well. He'd just killed two birds with one stone, hadn't he? In his search for Ellie, he'd stumbled upon another woman who'd conveniently run away from him.

The last time he'd seen Vivian was at Ellie's engagement

party, when he'd had his tongue in her mouth and his hands on her tits. He wasn't sure how they'd even ended up in each other's arms. A little too much champagne on both their parts, of course, but he knew it was more than that.

Maybe it was wrong to lust over a woman almost fifteen years his senior, but damn it, he'd been attracted to Vivian from the moment he met her. He was twenty-six, just opening up his law practice, and Vivian, well, she was forty and the sexiest woman he'd ever seen. A woman who also happened to be dropping her twenty-year-old daughter off at college. Josh hadn't asked her out simply because he knew she'd say no, but after that explosive kiss they'd shared two years later...he'd hoped something more might come of it. It hadn't.

After a two-month love affair with Vivian's answering machine, he'd finally learned from Viv's daughter that her mother had left town. Not the type of man to chase after a woman who obviously didn't want him, Josh gave up. Put Vivian Kendrick out of his mind and tried to move on. Even dated a few women in his quest to erase his feelings for her.

He thought he'd succeeded, that he no longer had a single residual emotion left for Vivian.

Obviously he'd thought wrong.

"Boss?"

He lifted his head and found Alice in the doorway again. "Yes?"

"I just wanted to let you know I'm leaving for the night." She hesitated. "Is everything all right? You look kind of, I don't know, flustered."

"Everything's fine." Then, as an afterthought, he added, "Actually, no, something came up. I need to go out of town. When you come in tomorrow, could you please cancel my appointments for the next week or so?"

"I'll do it first thing in the morning."

After Alice left, Josh leaned forward and grabbed the papers she'd left on his desk. He scanned the first one thoughtfully. San Valdez. Sounded like a nice little town. Too bad there was nothing nice about it.

He didn't know what had gotten into his sister but he wasn't about to let her get away with dancing in some sleazy burlesque show. Though Luke was probably one of the few people who knew how to control Ellie, Josh wasn't sure his best friend could do this alone.

Pushing the chair back, he stood up. It was settled. He'd fly down to San Valdez tomorrow, just to keep an eye on things and get a handle on the situation.

It had nothing to do with the fact that Vivian was there. Of course not. That would just be ridiculous. Pathetic, even. *Nope, doesn't matter that Viv's there.*

He was still trying to convince himself of that as he left the office and headed for the elevator.

og

Ellie spotted Luke the second he walked into the club. Instantly, she straightened her back, squared her shoulders, and lifted her chin in preparation for a fight.

He was here to coerce her to go home again, and no way would she give in to his bullying. No matter how good he looked right now, in his faded jeans and blue polo shirt. She wasn't going to let him push her around.

She usually performed two shows a night, one earlier in the evening, the second around ten and lasting until midnight, when the club was at full capacity. The first show had just ended, and there had been no doubt in her mind that Luke would be showing up soon. So she'd dashed to the dressing room after the performance and quickly changed into her regular clothes, then scrubbed all the makeup from her face. She'd have to reapply all the face gook when she came back to the club for the second show, but the hassle was worth it. This time she wanted to be comfortable when Luke ordered her around. It was hard to be taken seriously when you wore nothing but a corset.

"Is that him?" Vivian murmured, following Ellie's gaze.

The two women stood at the bar, their eyes trained on the darkened doorway of Vivian's club. At a nearby table, a group of rowdy locals filled the room with loud laughter and slurred chatter, but Ellie barely heard them. Her gaze was focused on the dark-haired man who'd just walked through the door.

She nodded. "Yep. My brother's henchman."

Appreciation filled Vivian's gaze. "If I were twenty years younger, I'd definitely fuck him."

"Viv!"

"Well, I would." Vivian made a tsking sound. "It's such a shame that he's so hot."

"Why is that a shame?"

"Because I'm supposed to dislike him. He's trying to take my favorite dancer away."

"Don't worry, Viv, I'm not going anywhere."

From across the room, Luke spotted her and began making his way toward the bar. His strides were long, determined. As determined as the look in his silver-gray eyes.

"Hello, Elenore," he drawled when he reached the two women.

"Lucas," she said in a cool voice. "Nice to see you again."

She held his gaze, and as usual, neither of them wanted to be the first to look away.

Vivian cleared her throat. "Hello. I'm Vivian, the owner of this place."

Looking reluctant, Luke broke the gaze and turned his head. "The owner, huh? So you're the one who lured Ellie away from ballet and into the world of *jazz*."

Vivian blinked, and then glanced at Ellie. "You're right, he *is* grumpy." Tossing her long blonde hair over her shoulders, she shot Luke a pointed look before wandering off.

"Didn't you used to have a way with the ladies?" Ellie said, smiling sweetly at him.

"Used to?" He looked insulted. "Still do."

"Really? Because Viv doesn't shoot dirty looks very often."

He ignored the comment. "Are you ready?"

"Ready for what?"

"Dinner."

He slung his hands in the pockets of his snug-fitting jeans, and her betraying eyes briefly rested on his firm, denim-clad thighs. He filled out a pair of jeans nicely. Too nicely.

She set her jaw. "I'm not hungry."

"Well, I am."

"So have dinner alone."

She knew she was being difficult, but she had the right. Luke, on the other hand, had absolutely no right showing up in San Valdez and ordering her to leave. For the first time in months, she was starting to feel good again. About herself. About her life. Ever so slowly, she'd begun to put everything behind her, all the devastating blows she'd received after the car accident.

And Luke wanted her to go home, to relive it all? No, thank you. He didn't run her life. Neither did her brother. And the two of them would need to learn that. The hard way, for all she cared.

"Ellie, it's eight o'clock and I haven't eaten because I've been waiting for your damn show to finish. Whether you like it or not, you're coming to dinner with me. And I'll be nice. You can choose the restaurant."

Deciding to pick her battles, she chewed on her lower lip. "Okay. There's this great seafood restaurant a few miles from here. It's right on the beach."

She saw Luke's jaw twitch. "You know I hate seafood."

Smirking, she said, "Well, that's what I feel like eating. Take it or leave it."

Leave it.

"Fine, let's go."

Ten minutes later, they walked into The Crab Conch, a tiny establishment situated on the white sand of Valdez Beach. The restaurant's patio opened up onto the sand, only a few yards from the rippling blue-green ocean. Ellie had always loved the coast, though she wasn't much into water sports, nor was she that big on swimming. What she loved was the sounds and the smells, the feel of hot sand beneath her bare feet and the way the salty breeze kissed her face. The soothing motion of the tide as it swelled toward the shore and then retreated, nature's own little seesaw.

The water looked calm this evening, sparkling under the dusky sky, and a warm, gentle wind snaked through the air and lifted Ellie's loose brown hair.

If she were with anyone other than Luke Russell, she might have enjoyed the romantic atmosphere.

"Here you are," the waitress announced, seating them at a table overlooking the shore.

Ellie jumped into the chair before Luke could play the chivalrous knight and pull it out for her, and then accepted a menu from the waitress. They ordered their drinks, and the waitress hurried off, leaving them alone.

"Everything on the menu looks delicious," she said cheerfully, glancing at Luke.

He examined the dishes listed on the plastic sheet and wrinkled his nose. She almost felt bad for bringing him here, knowing how much he disliked seafood.

But for showing up unannounced and making demands on her, he deserved to choke back a few clams.

"I guess I'll go with the Caesar salad," he muttered, setting down the menu.

Guilt tugged at her belly. Why did he have to look so appealing when he was dejected?

The waitress returned to take their meal orders, and after Ellie had ordered a lobster dinner, she hid a smile as Luke requested his salad.

The waitress seemed surprised. "That's it? A big man like you will be satisfied with a small salad?"

Ellie's spine stiffened at the flirtatious tone of the waitress's voice. Now that she looked at the woman, she realized she was really pretty. Gorgeous, actually, with long blonde hair, wide blue eyes and a pair of enormous breasts that made Ellie glance down at her own chest ruefully.

This woman was flirting with Luke. The nerve of her. For all she knew, Ellie was his girlfriend. Maybe they were out on a date, celebrating their tenth anniversary.

"Salad's the only thing on the menu I like," Luke answered,

his tone light, and damned if it wasn't sexy.

The waitress glanced at Ellie as if to say, *How dare you bring him here when he doesn't like seafood?* Then she returned her gaze to Luke.

"We have some burgers in the kitchen," she said, her voice sounding breathy to Ellie's ears. "Mostly for the staff, but I'm sure I can talk one of the cooks into grilling one up for you."

"Are you sure it's no trouble?"

The woman giggled. "Oh, it's no trouble at all. I'll run to the kitchen right now with your order."

"Thanks, sweetheart."

Sweetheart?

He winked at the waitress, who giggled again before rushing off like she was running the Boston marathon.

"Wasn't that nice of her?" Luke said with a lazy grin.

Ellie shook her head. "How do you do that?"

"Do what?"

"Make every woman fall at your feet. I've been here dozens of times and no one's ever offered to fix me something off the menu."

She tried not to let her irritation show. She'd seen Luke in action before, how one smile from him made women swoon. She'd always known Luke was a ladies man, and it had never annoyed her before. So why now? Why had seeing Luke flirt with that waitress made her feel all...troubled?

"I bet if you showed up in your dance costume you'd get a thing or two. A free meal. Maybe more."

She shot him a glare. "Would you stop implying that what I wear during the performance is trashy?"

"It isn't?"

"No."

She wanted to wipe that tiny little grin off his mouth. She wished Josh had never sent Luke to find her. She hadn't minded her brother's meddling growing up; she knew he was overprotective because he loved her, because he wanted to take care of her since their parents weren't there to do it. Yet since the car accident, Josh had started to smother her.

The car accident. Everything always came back to that damn accident. She wished she'd never decided to surprise Scottie at his office that day. If she'd just stayed in their condo and waited to tell him the good news when he got home from work, she wouldn't have been hit by that drunk driver. She wouldn't have had a miscarriage. She wouldn't have lost everything.

God, she didn't even want to think about it anymore. She'd been doing fine in this little town, away from the memories. Until Josh had decided to run her life again.

"Will you just make it easy on the both of us and come home?"

Luke's quiet voice snapped her from her thoughts. "This is my home now," she answered.

"You belong in San Francisco."

She wanted to scream. How did he know where she belonged?

"You should be thinking about settling down, having a family," he added.

"I'm only twenty-four," she protested.

"You were ready to settle down two years ago. With Scott." Luke paused. "Did I ever tell you I was sorry he broke off the engagement?"

"No."

His eyes softened. "Well, I am sorry."

"I don't want to talk about this." She couldn't hide the pain in her eyes, but Luke, thankfully, didn't comment on it.

"What do you want to talk about then?"

"When are you leaving?"

"I'm not. Next question." He crossed his arms over his broad chest.

She sighed. "Fine. What have you been up to these past couple of years?"

"Not much. Just working."

"Still a bodyguard?"

He nodded, and she couldn't control the rush of warmth that flooded her belly. Luke the bodyguard. She'd always thought his profession was so sexy. And it suited him. He was big and strong and masculine. It made sense that he earned his living protecting people.

"Any interesting assignments?" She suddenly smiled. "Taken a bullet for an actress lately?"

She was rewarded by a rumble of laughter from him. "Don't remind me of that," he said with a groan.

She laughed, almost as hard as the first time she'd learned that he'd thrown himself in front of Lucy Kincaid on the red carpet of a premiere. A man had darted out from the crowd, holding a gun, and Luke hadn't hesitated to risk his own life for Kincaid. The weapon, however, had turned out to be nothing more than a paint gun, and Ellie still remembered seeing Luke on the evening news, covered in green paint.

"I was actually assigned to a senator last month," he said. "Pretty tame. But the guy did have a few strange fetishes."

"Like what?" she asked, curious.

"He liked feet. Used to drag me to a thousand shoe stores a

33

day to watch people try on shoes."

She made a face, but laughed again. "I always liked hearing your work stories," she admitted.

"I always liked telling you."

Their eyes locked, and for one brief moment Ellie thought she saw a flash of desire in his gray eyes. Then she quickly shrugged away the thought. Desire? No way. Luke had never seen her as anything more than Josh's pesky kid sister.

"Here's your burger."

The waitress approached the table and placed Luke's dinner in front of him as if she were presenting him with an elaborate Thanksgiving feast. Then, without even glancing in Ellie's direction, she dropped the plate of lobster in front of her before smiling down at Luke again.

Trying not to roll her eyes, Ellie reached for her fork. The waitress lingered at the table as if she were waiting for Luke to say something more. Instead, he just thanked her and gave her another wink.

Once the waitress left, Ellie finally rolled her eyes.

"What was that for?" Luke said, glancing at her.

"That woman was practically undressing you with her eyes."

He shrugged. "Yeah."

"Yeah?" she echoed. "God, you're still as conceited as ever."

"And you're still a pest."

"But a cute pest," she corrected.

Luke's gaze briefly lowered to her breasts before returning to her face. "I'll give you that," he conceded.

Heat spilled over her cheeks. Had he just checked her out? Or had she imagined him looking at her breasts?

She speared some salad with her fork and chewed on a mouthful of lettuce. What on earth was happening here? Why was she having dinner with Luke?

After he'd left her dressing room last night, she'd been determined to find a way to make him leave. Luke was as stubborn as they came, but even he had his weak spots. She was well aware of the tight-knit friendship between Luke and her brother, and if Josh had called in a favor, Luke wouldn't hesitate to help out. But she could work around Luke's loyalty, if she just did something that would make him go running. Riling him up didn't seem to be working, so she'd need to find another route.

What she couldn't do was sit here in this restaurant and act like they were two old friends catching up. She didn't want him to get too comfortable here. She wanted him to go away, plain and simple.

She watched as he took a bite of his burger and wondered what it would take to make him leave. She briefly considered paying him—she had plenty of money left over from her parents' life insurance settlement—but she knew Luke wouldn't take her money.

"So, how did you meet Vivian?" He reached for the beer he'd ordered and took a long swig.

"Viv? She's Tanya's mother."

"Tanya...your roommate in college?"

She nodded. "I called Tanya after the—" she swallowed, "—accident. I told her I needed to find work. So she gave me her mom's number and Viv offered me a job dancing at her club."

A serious look crossed Luke's rugged features, and she couldn't help but admire his handsome face. God, why did he have to be so good-looking? She'd always loved his proud forehead, his strong, defined jaw and wide, sexy mouth. And

35

that dimple in his chin. She'd spent too many nights, back when she was a teenager, thinking about that dimple.

"Are you okay?"

Her cheeks flushed. "I'm fine. Why do you ask?"

"I mean, since the accident. How are you...feeling?"

All the muscles in her body tensed. The way he'd said that, it was almost like he knew about the pregnancy. Anger coursed through her in waves. Had Josh told him about the baby? She'd asked her brother not to breathe a word of it to anyone. The only people who knew she'd been pregnant were Scottie and her brother. Since she'd miscarried, she hadn't felt it was anyone's business.

If Josh had told Luke...

"I'm feeling fine," she snapped.

Luke looked taken aback. "No need to snap at me. I just wanted to know if your foot is all healed."

Her foot. Relief thawed her anger. Of course, he was referring to the foot she'd broken.

"It's fine. All better."

"So why didn't you return to the ballet company?" Luke said, his voice rough.

A lump of bitterness formed in the back of her throat, making it difficult to breathe. It had taken months for the reality of her situation to sink in, and even now, she still couldn't believe that she'd never dance ballet again.

For two very smart men, neither Josh nor Luke had figured out that her broken foot had rendered her useless. She'd broken three toes in the accident, as well as her ankle and heel, and torn her Achilles tendon. She'd never be able to dance *en pointe* again. Sure, she could strut around the stage to jazz, but her ballet career had officially ended the second that drunk driver had collided into her car.

Tears pricked at her eyes, and it was all she could do not to burst into sobs. All she'd ever wanted was to be a ballerina. A prima ballerina. Getting a job as a corps member with the Hartford Ballet Company had been the proudest moment of her life. In a few years, she could have been dancing the lead in *Swan Lake*. *The Nutcracker*. She could have lived out her dreams, the dreams her mother had had for her.

But all those dreams had deflated after the accident. Each and every one of them.

"Ballet doesn't interest me anymore," she lied, blinking back her tears.

"Ellie."

She met his gaze. "What?"

"Come back with me."

The fork dropped out of her hands and landed on her plate with a loud clatter. "Please, Luke, just stop."

"Ellie—"

"No, you don't get it, do you? This is my life now. I'm happy here. I like this town. I like the people here. I'm not going back."

"Why not?"

Because I have nothing to go back to.

"I just told you why. So please, leave me alone."

"I can't." He sounded unhappy.

"What'll it take to get you to go?" she demanded, challenging him with her eyes. "Money? The promise that I'll be okay? How about—"

A thought flew into her head, making her stop midsentence.

There was only one thing that had ever made Luke Russell

so uncomfortable he backed down.

Me.

He'd always been so determined to view her as nothing more than Josh's little sister. Whenever he'd started to notice she was more than that, that she was a red-blooded woman, he'd shut her out.

She thought about her eighteenth birthday, when they'd danced together at her party, the way he'd barely looked at her. She'd worn her new strapless mini-dress, and it had been obvious that Luke was trying hard to remain unaffected. He'd left early that night, and it was months before she'd seen him again.

Then she remembered the way he'd looked at her in her dressing room last night, after he'd torn her robe open. He'd liked what he'd seen, she was sure of it.

And she could use that against him.

"I told you, Ellie. I'm not leaving without you. You might as well accept it."

Accept it? No way. She was finally beginning to put the past behind her. She'd resigned herself to the fact that the future in store for her wasn't the one she'd always imagined.

And nobody, not even Luke, would make her face the pain again.

As if a light bulb lit up over her head, Ellie glanced at Luke, her eyes taking on a glint of determination. Then, clearer than if it had been written in the sky, she knew what she had to do.

And boy, was it going to be fun.

Chapter Three

"So how is this going to work?" Vivian asked the next afternoon, sipping on her piña colada.

Ellie bit her lip. "I'm not really sure yet. But trust me, it'll work."

The two women sat in the backyard of Ellie's small bungalow, though in this case, backyard actually meant beach. Situated a few yards from the shoreline, the quaint little house had found a place in her heart the second she'd seen it. So different from her San Francisco condo, a high-security, cookie-cutter apartment on the fifteenth floor, where breathing in fresh air meant facing her fear of heights and stepping onto the balcony. Here, all she had to do was open the back door and the scent of salt, ocean and coconut just drifted in.

After she'd moved in, she'd purchased a white wicker patio set that she positioned right on the sand. The legs of the chairs sank into the sand a little, but there was nothing more relaxing than sitting out here on her evenings off, eating dinner while listening to the sound of the waves lapping against the shore and the gulls squawking in the distance.

Vivian came over at least a couple times a week for lunch, since Ellie didn't own a car and was not interested in doing so. She hadn't driven since the accident that took her baby and ballet career and the thought of sitting behind the wheel again made the back of her neck break out in a cold sweat. Thankfully, Vivian understood, and stopping by Ellie's bungalow had become a routine for her.

Despite the twenty-year age difference, Ellie had come to rely on Vivian's friendship. Not only did she owe her big time for giving her a job, but she'd also grown to depend on Vivian's gentle humor and practical advice.

Today, though, she didn't like the advice being dished out.

"I think you're going to get in over your head," Vivian said.

"Why do you think that?"

"Let's just say that Luke Russell is fire, and you're playing with him."

Ellie rolled her eyes as she reached for her glass of lemonade. "Playing with fire? Come on, I've known Luke for more than half my life. He's harmless."

Vivian shot her a wary glance. "Really?"

"Yes."

No.

All right, so Luke Russell was most definitely *not* harmless. A part of her wondered if she'd ever really gotten over him. She'd always told herself her attraction for Luke was just a silly teenage crush, and when she'd fallen head over heels for Scott Whelan during her senior year of high school, she'd thought she'd gotten Luke out of her system for good.

But now that he'd stampeded back into her life like an angry bull, she wondered if maybe her desire for him had always been there, just waiting to rise up and break through the surface. She wasn't in love with the man. She was just drawn to him. Physically drawn to him.

And no matter how many times she tried to convince herself that seducing Luke would be a piece of cake, she still didn't buy it.

Viv was right. Luke was fire.

And when you played with fire, you got burned.

"Okay, let's talk this through," Vivian said in her usual, no-nonsense tone.

"Talk away," Ellie answered with a grin.

"So you want Luke to leave town, but he won't go unless you come with him."

"We already know this part."

"But the guy's stubborn. He can't be paid off, and he doesn't listen to reason."

"No, no, he doesn't," Ellie said, rueful.

"So the only way to make him go is to scare him away."

"Yep."

Vivian met her eyes. "How are you so sure seducing him will achieve that? What if he *wants* to be seduced?"

"Oh, believe me, Luke doesn't want to be seduced. Especially by me."

Because I'm nothing more than Josh's kid sister.

"Do you plan on having sex with him?"

Ellie choked on her lemonade. "Viv!"

It was hard to believe that the gorgeous blonde sitting in front of her had an adult daughter. Vivian didn't act or look like a forty-four year old, and Ellie still had a tough time accepting the woman she'd grown close to was the mother her college roommate Tanya had always complained about.

Talking about sex with someone's mother seemed...wrong.

"It's a valid question," Vivian said in her defense. "Seduction and sex go hand in hand."

Seduction and sex. The words brought a barrage of sensual

visuals to Ellie's brain. Images of Luke. Naked. Lying in a tangle of sheets. Looking at her with those smoldering eyes. Running his big hands up and down her—

Focus.

"I'm not going to sleep with him. I'm just going to...tease him," she finally said. "Tease him until he gets so uncomfortable he can't wait to be out of here."

"And if it backfires?"

"How can it backfire?"

"He can give in to your teasing."

"He won't." Her voice was firm.

"Really?" Vivian gave a sly grin. "I've never known a man to pass up what a pretty girl is offering."

"That's the thing," Ellie insisted. "Luke doesn't see me as a pretty girl. He sees me as Josh's little sister."

"And if his view changes? If he realizes how drop-dead gorgeous you are?"

Ellie flushed. "Thanks for the compliment. But he won't."

Vivian let out a long sigh. "I don't want you to get hurt. You've been through enough these past six months."

"I won't get hurt."

"I hope you're right, kiddo."

Luke stood in the center of room number eleven of the Lucky Strikes Motel, the one and only place to stay in town. He hung up the phone and stared at the receiver for a good two minutes, wondering what just happened.

See you in twenty minutes!

Ellie's cheerful, melodic voice floated around in his head,

bringing with it a spark of suspicion. No doubt about it, she was up to something.

When he'd dropped her back at the club after last night's dinner, the farewell hug she'd given him was so full of warmth and affection that his guard instantly soared up. Ellie never hugged him, and no matter how good her lithe body felt in his arms, he'd been wary. Still was.

She'd just called and invited him to join her for an afternoon swim, her tone so light and breezy that the guard he'd briefly let down shot up another ten feet.

What was the little spitfire planning?

Luke walked over to the rickety wood dresser and rummaged around in the top drawer for his swim trunks. After he'd stripped off his boxers, he pulled the trunks up to his hips, his mind running.

She wanted a swim?

Or had she come up with a plan?

She has a plan.

Okay, so that was indisputable. Ellie Dawson always had an ace or two up her sleeve. Like in college, when Josh had refused to release funds from her trust fund to allow her to go on a coed singles cruise. Rather than giving in, Ellie took a month off from her classes and worked full-time at a frozen yogurt stand to save up the money. And the kicker—she'd convinced her professor to count the job as extra credit.

Oh, she definitely had a plan, and it obviously involved him. She'd made it clear she didn't want him in this town, and if he knew Ellie, the wheels in her head were working overtime looking for a way to get rid of him.

He reached for the sunglasses sitting on the dresser and pushed them on top of his head. Then he sighed.

Damn, he wasn't in the mood for games. He'd endured too many of Robin's games these past few months, had suffered enough manipulation to last a lifetime. Why did women always feel the need to play games?

You won't lose this time.

He thought about the last time he'd seen his ex-girlfriend, when Robin's final lie floated to the surface and slapped him in the face like a splash of ice-cold water. The betrayal still resonated in his blood, slithered through his system like a hefty dose of arsenic. But hell, at least he'd learned his lesson. He'd strayed from his bachelor lifestyle, committed himself to one woman, only to have it all blow up in his face.

He wasn't about to make that mistake again.

Luke grabbed the keys for the SUV he'd rented and headed for the door. No, he wouldn't lose this time. He wasn't going to let another woman play him for a fool.

Even if that woman was Ellie.

Fifteen minutes later, he pulled up in the driveway of her little pink bungalow. He stared at the house, noting just how *Ellie* it was. Pink and sweet and easy on the eyes.

He got out of the car and strode up the flower-lined front walk. There was no doorbell, so he rapped his knuckles against the sleek white door, waiting. When she didn't answer after his first few knocks, he called out, "Ellie?"

"I'm out back!"

Her voice drifted in the wind, and he made his way around the bungalow toward the beachside backyard. When he spotted her, she was sprawled on a lounge chair, wearing a yellow halter top and denim shorts.

"Hi," she called as he came near.

"Hi, yourself." He sank on the beach chair next to hers and

stretched out his legs.

He couldn't stop himself from giving her a long once-over. Nobody could argue that Ellie wasn't cute. A pair of oversized sunglasses sat perched on her dainty nose, and she'd tied her hair up in a messy ponytail. His eyes briefly rested on her bare legs, admiring the sleek, golden tone of her skin. She looked young, healthy and really, really good.

Josh's sister.

Those two words were all it took, the same two words he'd used almost as a mantra each time he'd found his thoughts drifting into forbidden territory. Josh was the best friend he'd ever had, and he wasn't about to mess around with his sister.

Of course, that didn't mean he hadn't wondered what it would be like to date Ellie. She was so different from the women he typically went out with. Sassy, sarcastic, the kind of woman who never backed down from a challenge. He'd been with all types of women. Strong CEO types, ditzy supermodel types, complacent yes types, but never someone like Ellie.

Truth was, there wasn't anyone like her. She was one of a kind.

"Beautiful day, isn't it?" she chirped, sliding up the chair so that she sat cross-legged.

Her feet were bare, and her shiny pink toenails made his groin stir. He pictured her wearing those dainty little ballet slippers and his groin stirred some more. He'd always thought ballerinas were extremely sexy.

Josh's sister.

"It's a very nice day." He noticed his voice sounded hoarse.

"I'm glad you came over for a swim. Viv was here a while ago, but she hates the ocean. She's terrified of it, actually."

Luke lifted a brow. "Vivian, terrified? Seems like she has

nerves of steel."

"She does." Ellie shrugged. "But ever since she watched a documentary on currents and riptides, she's boycotted the ocean."

"I'm actually surprised you called me." He searched her big blue eyes for a reaction, hoping she'd reveal a hint of her true intentions, but her gaze remained innocent. Too innocent?

"I hate swimming alone," she replied. "And since you're refusing to get out of here, I figured we could spend some time together."

He forced his eyebrows to stay in place and not shoot upwards. She wanted to spend time with him? Now he was certain she had something up her sleeve.

"That sounds terrific," he said, matching her cheerful tone.

If she wanted to play games, he was more than ready to play back.

"So, ready to take a dip?"

No, he wasn't. He wanted to sit here next to her and do some digging. Find out why she'd suddenly decided to welcome him with open arms. But the afternoon sun beating down on his head already caused beads of sweat to dot his forehead, and the blue-green water lapping against the white sand looked mighty inviting.

"Sure," he finally said.

Luke stood up and unbuttoned his shirt, then dropped it on the chair. As he took a step forward, Ellie's voice stopped him.

"Would you rub some suntan lotion on my back first?" she said, her big eyes focusing on his. "I burn easily."

His throat went dry. "Uh..."

"Please, Luke? You don't want me to get a sunburn, do

you?"

He found his voice. "Of course I don't."

"Good."

He thought he saw a whisper of a smile—a satisfied smile—sweep over her mouth, but he must have imagined it, because when he looked at her again her lush lips were closed in a straight line.

"Is that what you're wearing in the water?" he asked, gesturing to her shorts and halter.

This time she did smile. "I've got my suit underneath."

She jumped up from the chair and reached for the tie that held her halter together. Quickly, she undid the knot and pulled the top over her head. The second she did that, not only did thick cotton fill his entire mouth, but a rush of heat pooled in his groin.

A string bikini. She wore a fucking string bikini.

He tried not to stare, but his foolish eyes kept darting toward her chest. Small, perky breasts barely covered by the tiny green triangles of her bikini top. He was pleased to see that he'd been right—the corset *had* made her breasts appear larger.

But those small luscious mounds still looked just as inviting.

"Here."

He unglued his gaze from her, wondering if she'd caught him staring. If she had, she didn't comment on it, just handed him a tube of sunscreen and flopped down on the chair, offering her back to him.

He stared at the flimsy string at her back and noted that he could probably tear it off with his teeth with no trouble.

Josh's sister.

"That's the only thing I hate about living on the beach," she said. "My skin is far too sensitive. Two minutes in the sun and I turn into a tomato."

The sensitive comment stayed in his head. He wondered which parts of her were most sensitive. Her lips? Her nipples?

"Luke? The sunscreen?"

He forced his mind out of his swim trunks and unscrewed the cap of the tube. Squirting a glob of sunscreen into his hands, he rubbed his palms together and stared at her golden skin.

He took a breath.

Then he touched her.

The second he made contact with her delicate shoulder blades, a jolt of electricity coursed through his body and settled in his crotch. Damn, her skin felt like silk.

"So, are you still with the same bodyguards-to-the-rich-and-famous agency?"

It was impossible to hold a normal conversation while his hands rubbed sunscreen on her back. He managed a short, "Uh-huh."

Ellie suddenly leaned back, filling his palms with more of that soft skin. "Mmmm, that feels good. You should give up life as a bodyguard for a career as a masseur."

Josh's sister. Josh's sister.

The mantra grew louder in his head, desperate, as he fought back a barrage of sensual thoughts.

You think this feels good? Well, come to bed with me. You'll feel even better.

He swiftly dropped his hands from her back and wiped the excess sunscreen on his own chest. Okay, this was bad. Normally he exercised a hefty dose of restraint, yet in the past few seconds, he'd lost every bit of control he'd ever managed to maintain around Ellie.

"Okay, all done." His voice sounded too high to his ears, and he cleared his throat. "Let's go for that swim."

Cold water. That's what he needed. Being submerged in cold water would shoot some sense into him.

Ellie stood up and flashed him another endearing smile. "Thanks for doing my back. Let me just get my legs before we go in."

She wiggled out of her denim cut-offs, revealing a pair of green bikini bottoms. He almost sighed with relief. High-cut, but modest. He could handle these bottoms, no problem.

He watched as she slathered sunscreen on her bare legs, and then tossed the tube on the sand.

"I'll race you," she said with a grin.

He was about to accept the challenge and start dashing down the sand, but the second she took a step forward, all the breath sucked out of his lungs with one swift whoosh.

She was wearing a thong.

"Are you coming?" She broke into a slow jog, smiling at him over her shoulder.

All he could do was stand there, stare at her ass and will away his erection.

This was really bad.

He swallowed, unable to tear his gaze from her butt, and it wasn't until he saw her diving cleanly into the waves that he snapped out of his lust-filled stupor.

Okay, no big deal. Just a thong. Lots of women wear thongs. Some don't wear anything at all. You can overcome this.

With a breath, he jogged down the sand toward the water's edge. Ellie was already a few yards out, languidly floating on her back.

"Slowpoke!" she teased.

He dove into the water, grateful for the cold rush that filled his body. As he swam toward Ellie, his desire slowly dissolved, much to his relief. By the time he reached her, he'd almost forgotten all about the dental-floss string nestled between her ass cheeks.

"Finally," she said as he approached her with slow strokes. "You've lost your edge, Russell."

He sent a small splash of seawater in her direction. "You cheated."

"How did I cheat?"

"You didn't count us off. You can't have a race without a count." He neglected to mention the real reason for his less than speedy entrance.

Luke watched as she did a leisurely backstroke, her shapely legs kicking through the water. He realized this was the first time he'd ever been alone with Ellie. It was incredible to think it, that he'd known her for fifteen years, and they'd never spent more than a few moments alone. He wondered why that was, but got his answer quickly as Ellie smiled at him again and her face lit up.

Being alone with her was dangerous, which was why he'd always made sure someone else was around whenever he was with Ellie. He could trace it back to her eighteenth birthday, when he'd first realized that Elenore Dawson had become a woman. A beautiful, alluring, sexy woman.

A woman who was totally off-limits.

His dating track record was impressive. He'd been with many women, and his past encounters all had one commonality—they were brief. He wasn't ashamed of his love 'em and leave 'em past. In his line of work, settling down wasn't really an option, as he constantly traveled the country, moving from assignment to assignment. When he *was* home he tried to spend as much time as possible with his father, who'd been a mess ever since Luke's mom died ten years ago.

Making a commitment to one woman was nearly impossible considering his conflicting loyalties. He'd learned that the hard way with Robin. While her betrayal still infuriated him, he found himself unable to let her shoulder all the blame for their break-up. Robin had wanted him to devote every second of the day to her, she'd wanted full and total control of his heart, and that's the one thing he hadn't been able to give her.

He'd never felt guilty about the casual affairs he engaged in, but he knew that, with Ellie, casual wouldn't cut it. Josh would kill him if he got involved with Ellie, if he kept things with her light and deprived her of a real future, a family, his heart. So he'd never let himself act on his attraction to her. Hell, he hadn't even been sure there was an attraction.

Until now.

"The water feels wonderful, doesn't it?"

She swam over to him again, brushing damp strands off her forehead as the water bobbed over her tanned shoulders.

"Yeah. I rarely have time for swimming anymore."

Treading water, she suddenly grinned. "Weren't you on your high school swim team?"

He suppressed a groan as he remembered the designated Speedo he'd had to wear back then. "Don't remind me. It was my dad's idea, not mine."

"I think Josh might have taken me to one of your meets." She splashed him. "Didn't you have to wear a g-string or something?"

He saw the playful twinkle in her blue eyes and glared at her. "No, it wasn't a g-string, Elenore."

51

A wave of laughter bubbled out of her throat. "Do you still have your g-string? Do you model it for your girlfriends?"

"Oh, that's it." With one swift move, he reached out and dunked her under the water, enjoying the shriek of surprise she let out before she went under.

She shot up to the surface, water sputtering from her mouth. "You're really going to get it, Russell!"

She launched herself at him, pressing her hands against his shoulders and trying to push him under. He fought against her attempts, until they were both laughing and spitting water from their mouths.

"Okay, okay, game over!" she cried out as he cupped his hands and shot a spray of salty water into her face. "I need to catch my breath."

As he watched her push her hair out of her eyes, he realized he was actually having a good time. So good a time that he'd forgotten all about his goal. What was he doing? He was supposed to bring her home, not frolic in the ocean with her.

"Let's go in," he suggested.

She looked disappointed, but she nodded. "Okay."

They swam toward the shore, and it wasn't until he saw her step onto the sand that he remembered.

The thong.

Don't look at her.

He diverted his gaze to his feet, and when she said, "Here's a towel," he finally looked up.

She'd wrapped a fluffy pink towel around her waist, thankfully shielding her barely-there bikini. As he dried off, he tried to regroup. All right, so she'd distracted him during that swim. And yeah, that sexy thong had made him reconsider telling his college friends that he was a boob man and made him realize he was most definitely an *ass* man.

But he was focused now. And ready to start pressuring her to go back. People always caved under pressure. You just needed the right amount, and they always caved. Ellie would be no exception.

"So, do you have a show tonight?" he asked, tossing the towel on the lounge chair.

She shook her head. "It's my night off."

Perfect. "So, you want to have dinner tonight?"

He saw the reluctance in her eyes. No matter how confident she'd been a few minutes ago, he knew she didn't want to have dinner with him again. Because she'd give in. They both knew she would.

"I can't," she said, running her fingers through her wet hair.

"Come on," he coaxed.

This would be easy. One more dinner, a few more guilt-trips about how much her brother missed her, and Ellie would be sitting next to him on a plane back to San Francisco.

"No, I really can't."

"Why not?" *She's getting desperate. She knows you'll win this little game.*

And then she threw him for a loop. "Because I have a date."

Chapter Four

I have a date.

Why, *why* had she said that?

Ellie collapsed on the plush white sofa in the center of the living room and let out the sigh she'd been holding. Luke had left only five minutes ago, but those five minutes, saying good-bye, walking him to his SUV, had been the longest of her life. Especially when he'd thrown in a few innocent questions about her *date*, questions she had no answers for.

As she'd watched him speed off, all her confidence had sped away with him.

No way could she beat Luke in a battle of wits. He could be sly, ruthless when he wanted, and he just oozed confidence. Sure, she'd had the upper hand for most of the afternoon—the string bikini had worked to her advantage—but she'd had to blow it by coming up with a ridiculous lie.

A date.

Ellie groaned. Where on earth would she find a date? If she knew Luke—and really, she could read him like a book—he'd undoubtedly show up at the club tonight, the location of her so-called rendezvous. No way would he stay away.

Okay, I can do this.

She rose from the couch and began pacing the hardwood floor. The living room was spacious and airy, the perfect place to think. Too bad her brain was mush. Had been that way the second Luke had shown up at her house today.

How she'd managed to get through the afternoon was beyond her. When Luke had taken off his shirt earlier, revealing his broad, golden chest, her knees had grown wobbly and her heart thudded in her chest. Why did he have to be so good-looking? Why did sex appeal pour out of him like lava from a volcano?

She cursed her brother for sending Luke here. Josh had tons of friends, why hadn't he sent Martin Hodges, his stuttering poker buddy? If Martin had been in that ocean with her today instead of Luke, she might have been able to focus.

Instead, she'd fought back wave after wave of desire until the ache had become unbearable. She thought about the way they'd played around in the water, the oddly gentle firmness of his touch when he'd grabbed her shoulders and dunked her in the waves. So many times she'd had to bite her lip to stop herself from begging him to kiss her.

Kiss him! When she should want him gone.

Her plan had seemed so simple, so easy to orchestrate. At least it seemed that way yesterday. Today she was a bundle of nerves, uneasy with the realization that scaring Luke off wouldn't be as simple as she'd thought. Doing it required control, and whenever Luke was around, all her self-control flew out the window.

Which provoked her to do stupid things. Like conjure up pretend dates. But really, how could she have survived another dinner with Luke? After the way her entire body throbbed at his mere proximity, seeing him again tonight hadn't been an option.

"Viv," she muttered, suddenly making a beeline for the

telephone.

Of course. If anyone could find her a man in less than three hours, it was Vivian.

Ellie dialed her boss's number and waited for Vivian's cheerful, "Hello?"

"Viv, it's me. I need your help." Her voice came out in a hurried rush.

"Ellie, I'm afraid I'm a little busy right now. The pool guy's here, trying to fix the filter. We think something's jamming it."

She paused. "The pool guy? How old is he?"

"I don't know. Twenty-seven, twenty-eight. Why?"

She took a breath. "Do you think he'll go out with me tonight?"

There was silence on the other end. Ellie could picture Vivian's perplexed expression, and if she weren't so desperate right now she might have laughed out loud. Trying to arrange a date with Viv's pool boy was probably the most absurd thing she'd ever done.

"Okay, what's going on?" Vivian finally asked. "What did you—"

Before Vivian could finish, the entire story spilled out of Ellie's mouth, starting with her swim with Luke and ending with the childish lie she'd told him.

"All right, honey." Vivian gave an audible sigh. "Let me talk to Miguel. Hold on."

Holding the phone to her ear, Ellie paced the room.

"Okay, I have good news and bad news. Pick your order," Vivian said a few moments later.

"Good news first."

"Miguel agreed to take you out tonight."

Relief flooded her chest. "And the bad news?"

"He's gay."

Hysterical laughter bubbled in her throat but she swallowed it back. Great, the only available bachelor she had, and he didn't like women. How would this ever work?

"But," Vivian added quickly, "he's very good at pretending he's straight. He should be a convincing date."

"Knowing Luke, he'll be at the next table, watching over us like a hawk. Miguel had better be convincing." Oh, God, she was in way over her head.

"Is this a bad time to reaffirm my notion that you're playing with fire?"

Ellie groaned. "Is there ever a good time to make me feel like an idiot?"

Vivian was laughing when she hung up the phone. If she had to pick one thing she loved about having Ellie living here in town—and there were many—it was that she made life exciting again. Not that Vivian was a believer of any of those silly sayings—*Life ends when you hit forty* being one, and her favorite, *Have a kid and kiss your life goodbye.*

A load of bull, of course. Some of her best memories were from recent years, and she certainly didn't regret having Tanya. Her daughter was the most important person in her life and always would be. Yet, since Tanya had moved off on her own, Vivian was having trouble adjusting. She'd been a mother for so long, now that her baby didn't need her anymore she didn't know what to do with herself. She'd worked as a medical receptionist in San Francisco, not because she had an all-consuming love for the job, but to put food on the table and pay for Tanya's college tuition. With Tanya out of the house and on her own, Vivian had quit the job and decided to really think about what she wanted to do with the rest of her life.

Moving to San Valdez hadn't even occurred to her until she ran into an old friend who happened to be the owner of the Dancehall. The man was eager to sell the club and the need to do something new prompted her to buy it from him. The move had also allowed her to get away from the newest complication in her life. Maybe it was taking the coward's way out, but hell, she deserved at least one act of cowardice in her life. She could've copped out years ago, when her parents had urged her to have an abortion once they found out she was pregnant. Instead, she'd ignored their advice, became a twenty-year-old single mother and worked her ass off to make ends meet. She hadn't taken the coward route then, but she sure as hell was entitled now.

"All fixed." Miguel's cheerful voice broke through her thoughts and brought on another chuckle.

Ellie would have a blast with him. Miguel had been working as her pool boy for two years and something about his slightly feminine Spanish accent and mischievous brown eyes sparked a deep fondness in Vivian. He really was a decent boy. She just hoped Luke Russell wouldn't eat him alive.

"Thanks, Miguel. I'll have a check for you next time you come by." She rose from the pool chaise she'd been lounging on and walked Miguel to the back gate. "Take care of my girl tonight, will you?"

He shot her a big smile. "I'll do my best. You know, this is the first date I've had in ten years."

She raised a brow, not quite believing him. "Really?"

His smile widened. "With a woman, of course."

Opening the door for him, she fought back another wave of laughter. Damn, maybe she ought to go into work tonight, if only to see the fireworks sure to explode.

After Miguel left, Vivian crossed the yard and climbed up the large cedar deck. She collected the sarong and magazine she'd left on the table, and then headed inside the house. Since her entire body was covered with tanning oil, she decided to take a shower before she settled down on the couch with a good book. She allowed herself one day a week to unwind and relax, and no matter how tempted she was to go to the club and take a front row seat to Ellie's date, she concluded it wasn't worth giving up her downtime.

"Poor Luke," she muttered to herself. The guy was barking orders at the wrong girl.

She reached for the strings holding her bikini top together and tugged on them. The top slid off, causing her breasts to drop a little, which in turn caused her to stifle a sigh. Ah, she longed for the days when her breasts had been so firm and perky she didn't even need to wear a bra. Or when those irritating stretch marks that had plagued her skin since giving birth had yet to exist. Oh well, she knew she still looked good. Slim waist, firm ass, wrinkle-free face. Sure, there were minor imperfections like the sagging breasts and stretch marks, but she could overlook those. With her non-existent sex life, it was doubtful anyone would see them anyway.

She took two steps toward the washroom when a loud knock rapped against the front door. *Now who the hell was that?* She paused for a moment, and then realized it was probably Ellie. No doubt a basket case over her date tonight.

Grinning to herself, Vivian walked to the door, having no qualms about covering her chest with one hand and throwing open the door with the other.

She regretted it instantly.

"Hi, Viv." His voice was deeper than she remembered. But still sexy. *He* was still sexy.

"Josh," she squeaked. She cringed. "What are you doing here?"

She lifted her other hand to her chest, feeling exposed and vulnerable as she stood there. Topless. A rush of heat coursed through her when his blue-eyed gaze swept over her upper body. A muscle twitched in his jaw but he remained expressionless save for the quick spark of suspicion in his eyes. "Am I interrupting something?" he asked coolly.

"What?" She caught the implication and found herself stuttering. "No, uh, of course not. I was about to hop in the shower."

His suspicion gave way to relief. "Oh." He hesitated. "Can I come in?"

She had no idea what to say. The word *no* bit at her tongue but she also wasn't thrilled about standing half-naked in front of her open door for the entire town to see. Finally she just nodded, wordlessly gesturing for him to come inside.

She closed the door behind them and turned slowly, looking at him. God, he was gorgeous. His dark hair was shorter now, almost a buzz cut, but it suited him, and the white button-down shirt he wore emphasized his broad chest and trim waist. He'd grown a slight beard too. The last time she'd seen him he'd been smooth and clean-shaven. Now dark stubble dotted his face, making him appear far older than he was.

But she knew better. He was young. *Much* too young. Fourteen years younger than her, to be exact.

"You look amazing, Viv." His voice jarred her from her scrutiny, but he didn't seem to mind that she was checking him out. He was doing the same, actually. Sweeping his gaze up and down her body before meeting her eyes.

Her reaction to his appreciative examination unnerved her.

Her nipples hardened against the hands covering them and she found herself growing wet as she stood there, looking into the eyes of the man she'd almost slept with.

"Thanks," she managed before taking a few jerky steps backwards. "I... Let me just put some clothes on."

Her legs felt shaky as she made for the bedroom, but she forced herself to appear calm. Josh couldn't know how much his nearness affected her.

In her room, she pulled random items of clothing out of the closet. Threw on a pair of jeans over her bikini bottoms and a black tank top over her bare breasts. Damn it, this was wrong. She shouldn't be attracted to this man. He was Ellie's brother. He was more than a decade younger than she was. He was...sinfully sexy.

Somehow during his sister's engagement party Vivian had wound up in his arms. Afterwards she'd decided it had just been the champagne. Oh, and the fact that she'd been celibate for three years at that point in time. She'd latched onto the first warm-bodied male and it hadn't mattered who said male happened to be. At least that's what she'd always told herself.

Now? Well, now she was rethinking her rationalization. One look at Josh Dawson and she was ready to go to bed with him. She wasn't drunk and she wasn't all that horny, so that meant...

She didn't even want to consider what that meant.

It took a few deep meditative breaths before she was ready to leave the room. When she did, she found Josh sitting on her couch, his hands clasped loosely over his lap. He glanced up when she entered, again eyeing her with that intense gaze she suspected was his trademark.

"So what brings you to town?" she asked, trying to sound cheerful. Before he could reply, she answered her own question.

"Ellie, of course."

When he nodded she was troubled by the pang of disappointment that hit her. It shouldn't bother her that he hadn't come to see her.

But it did.

"I want her to come home," Josh said in a firm tone.

Vivian sank into the armchair farthest from the leather sofa, hoping the distance between them would slow her racing pulse. "Isn't that why you sent Luke Russell?"

"I'm not sure he'll have any luck." Josh's features creased with frustration. "We both know how stubborn my sister can be."

She found herself grinning. "I would think you would've learned your lesson by now. You can't make Ellie do anything she doesn't want to do."

"No kidding." He looked rueful now as he met her eyes. "I need your help, Viv."

"Me?" she echoed in surprise. Her surprise quickly transformed into suspicion, which made itself known in the form of a sharp frown. "I'm not getting involved, Josh. No way will I join forces with you to control your sister. I happen to care about Ellie."

"And I don't?"

He raked his fingers through his dark hair and Vivian's fingers tingled in response. She still remembered how silky those short strands had felt between her fingers, when her arms had been twined around his neck and her hands tangled in his hair. She forced the memory away and tried to focus on the topic at hand. A difficult task when he sat just a few feet away from her.

"I love Ellie to death," he continued, sounding gruff and far too sweet for Vivian's comfort. "But she doesn't belong here. We both know that."

"She's a grown woman. She makes her own decisions."

"She should be at home. Dancing ballet again, dating again."

Vivian sighed. "You don't have a say in it. Ellie is the one to decide whether she dates, or whether she dances ballet again."

Anger flashed across his handsome face. "I see. So you think it's perfectly okay for my baby sister to be dancing in your strip club."

"My club is *not*—"

He cut her off, his voice sharp and furious. "How could you do that to her? Why the hell did you give her that job?"

"Because she asked me." Her own voice was quiet.

"You should've said no. Damn it, Viv! You had no right bringing Ellie down here. No right messing with her ballet career. No goddamned right screwing with her feelings, no, telling her how she's *supposed* to feel and—" He stopped abruptly, his lips tightening.

The silence that followed was deafening. It lasted just long enough for a river of guilt to flow down her chest and into her belly, where it swirled around like a violent eddy. They weren't talking about Ellie anymore, that much was blatantly obvious. What confused her was the look in his eyes. Anguished. Frustrated. Hurt.

Had she hurt him by leaving? She still felt bad about blowing him off the way she had. Not taking his phone calls, leaving town without letting him know. Not that she'd moved because of Josh. The thought of owning a nightclub had been genuinely exciting; the fact that it required her to leave San Francisco had just been an added bonus.

Josh Dawson was an attractive, charming, virile young man. He didn't need to be saddled with a forty-four-year-old single mom who'd probably be hitting menopause any year now. That's why she'd swiftly extinguished the flame that was determined to keep smoldering between them. She wouldn't have been able to live with herself if she'd deprived him of what he really needed—a serious committed relationship with a woman his own age.

But with his pain-tinged words still hanging in the air and that wounded flicker still awash in his eyes, she wondered if maybe she'd made a mistake.

"I never told you how to feel," she murmured, feeling like a teenager again as she avoided his gaze.

"Fine, I'll rephrase. You never gave me the *chance* to feel." An unmistakable splash of bitterness lined his voice.

"We both know that kiss was a mistake." She squared her shoulders, stood up and turned away from him. She couldn't look at him. Not unless she wanted him to see the truth in her eyes, which clearly conveyed the lack of conviction in her words. Kissing Josh hadn't been a mistake, not when it felt so right. The mistake would be letting that one kiss become something more.

"You're lying." She nearly jumped when she felt him come up behind her, his rough beard scratching the shell of her ear and tickling her skin. His voice lowered to a smoky pitch as he added, "That kiss was the best thing that ever happened to both of us."

She swallowed hard, gathered every ounce of self-control she possessed, then turned and took a few steps back. The passion glittering in Josh's eyes was enough to make her legs tremble. Enough to make her giddy with desire. But she couldn't bring herself to tell him he was right. Instead, she did the only thing she thought might put an end to this. Whatever *this* was. She changed the subject.

"What do you plan on doing about Ellie?"

She didn't need to be a brain surgeon to know he was disappointed. He obviously wanted to finish what he'd started, but to her relief he let it go. Oh, he'd bring it up again, that she knew, but for now he'd granted her a much-needed reprieve.

"I'm not sure yet," he replied, a distant look crossing his face. "But I don't want her or Luke to know I'm in town just yet. Which is why I came here."

Uneasiness crept up her throat. "What do you mean?"

"I need a place to stay." He must have caught her startled reaction because he quickly continued. "There's only one motel in this town and Luke checked into it. The next hotel is an hour's drive from here, so I figured I can best lay low if I stay with you."

Stay with her? And turn her home into a modern-day Garden of Eden, complete with temptation and forbidden fruit?

Oh God.

"What about Ellie?" she pointed out quickly, ignoring her pounding heart. "You think she won't know if you're in town?"

"She won't if you don't tell her."

Wonderful. Now he was not only asking to stay in her house, but he wanted her to lie to the girl who had become her best friend.

"What if she stops by for a surprise visit?"

"We both know Ellie doesn't own a car. And I doubt she'd be up to the walk, she lives across town. Chances are, she'll call you to pick her up if she wants to come over."

"She could take a cab." She was grasping at straws but the idea of Josh here, in her personal space, was far too daunting.

"Look, I know it might be an inconvenience but I really have no other options." He shrugged. "I need to keep an eye on my sister."

She managed to speak despite the lump lodged in her throat. "Josh…"

"Come on, Viv." He shot her a grin that was both charming and full of way too much sinful promise. "Do me this favor?"

She swallowed again. No, she gulped. Really hard. And then she wondered, how bad could it really be, letting him stay here? *How bad?* her conscience taunted. *Do you even have to think about it?*

She held back a sigh. Oh hell, letting Josh stay here would be disastrous and every part of her knew it. Her brain. Her body. Her heart.

Her mouth, on the other hand, had other ideas. Instead of a polite refusal, what came out of that irritating mouth was, "All right, you can stay."

A few hours later, Ellie paced the living room as she waited for her date to pick her up. Miguel had called ten minutes ago to say he was on his way, and despite the fact that this outing was nothing more than a childish charade, she was nervous.

It was times like these she desperately missed her mother. She'd been nine when her parents had died, but her memories of her mother were as vivid as if they'd happened just yesterday. She remembered all the times her mom had helped her with her homework, how she'd always given advice when Ellie fought with her friends, or when she'd developed her first crush on a boy in her fourth-grade class. And it had been her mother who'd encouraged her to take up ballet, when Ellie had fallen in love after seeing a Christmas performance of *The Nutcracker*.

She stopped pacing as hot tears stung her eyes. God, she missed her. She needed her so much right now. These six months had been hell, and if her mother were there she might have been able to help her through it all. Her mom would have been patient, supportive, unlike Josh, who was determined to fix everything. Like the toys he'd fixed for her when they were kids.

Too bad she couldn't be fixed. She was broken beyond repair.

A knock on the door pulled Ellie from her thoughts, and she blinked back the tears still welling in her eyes.

As she walked to the door, she squared her shoulders. Her mother was gone, so was the future she'd worked hard for, and as devastating as it was, she needed to be strong. She wouldn't let Luke drag her back to San Francisco like a stray kitten.

Pushing open the door, she pasted a big smile on her face. "Hi," she greeted her date.

Vivian's pool boy was a lot better looking than Ellie had expected. Taking in his light-brown skin, striking brown eyes and chiseled jaw, she almost forgot this was a farce as familiar first-date butterflies fluttered around in her stomach.

The reality of the situation, however, sunk in the second he opened his mouth and in a faint Spanish accent said, "Okay, girlfriend, tell me everything I need to know about this man we're supposed to make jealous."

Chapter Five

Luke shifted in his chair, keeping his eyes focused on the front doors of the Dancehall and trying to forget about the conversation he'd just had. Josh had called again demanding a progress report, and when Luke admitted he was still getting nowhere, Josh hadn't been pleased. The way he ranted and raved, it was Luke's fault Ellie still refused to come home. Didn't the guy know his own sister by now? Open the dictionary and you'd find Ellie Dawson's picture under the word "stubborn". Josh was an idiot if he didn't know that.

The worst part of the phone call came when Josh hinted he might come down to San Valdez, an absurd idea that had Luke swallowing back an incredulous retort. Josh showing up and barking orders would only infuriate Ellie. Knowing her, she'd slither away in the middle of the night and take off to another obscure town, which would require Luke to track her down. Again.

Luke had recommended Josh stay put, but considering the Dawson DNA was compiled primarily of genetic pigheadedness, he got the feeling his warnings would go unheeded.

Damn Dawsons. How did they both manage to wrap him around their little fingers?

Stifling a sigh, his gaze strayed once more to the door as a quick flash of movement caught his eye.

Shit. She'd been telling the truth.

He watched, frowning, as the couple entered the room. Hand-in-freaking-hand. Ellie's date was a tall, twenty-something guy with tanned skin and a head of wavy brown hair. He kind of looked like that singer, Enrique what's-his-last-name, which was odd, because he didn't think Ellie went for the Latin heartthrob type. Especially considering that Scott Whelan, her ex-fiancé, had been the All-American football quarterback, with blond hair, blue eyes and a set of straight white teeth that no doubt sparkled in the sunlight.

Luke moved his gaze to Ellie, trying not to notice how good she looked. She wore a short yellow dress that barely grazed her lower thighs, and her chocolate-brown hair flowed over her shoulders in shiny waves. Gripping Enrique's hand, she sauntered into the bar, her hips swaying.

Damn, where had she learned to walk like that? Had her stride always been this sultry, this blatantly seductive? And if so, how had he never noticed?

The couple seated themselves at a table in the far end of the room, right near the jukebox. Great. He'd never be able to hear what they said from all the way over here.

"Another beer?"

A tall, red-haired waitress approached his table, temporarily blocking his line of vision and shielding Ellie from view. "Yeah, sure, a beer. Maybe two." *Anything for you to move out of the way.*

The waitress scurried off just in time for Luke to get an eyeful of Ellie's shapely legs. Her skirt was hiked up, revealing one firm, tanned thigh. His fingers tingled with the urge to march over there, pull her skirt even higher, and run his hands along her soft skin.

Every part of him grew hot and hard at the thought.

Damn it, what was the matter with him? This was *Ellie*. Elenore Dawson, the girl he'd watched grow up. He blinked, hoping to direct his mind to the vision of her in her silver braces and pigtails, but his brain refused to comply. Instead, all he could see was that golden skin. Those luscious breasts and endless legs.

"That's so funny!"

Ellie's melodic laughter floated in his direction and settled between his legs. Fire began simmering in his blood, heating up all the parts that already ached for her. He watched as she leaned forward and touched her date's hand, and even from across the room he saw her dainty fingers trembling.

Was she nervous? According to Josh, she'd refused to date after Scott had broken off their engagement. Was this the first date she'd had since?

The waitress strolled up to his table again and deposited two beers. He gripped one bottle between his fingers. Ellie laughed again, louder this time, and she was gazing at her Latin lover as if he were the only man in the room.

Jealousy pricked Luke's insides. What he wouldn't give to have her look at him like that. In bed.

Josh's sister.

His jeans tightened over his erection, making him curse the mantra that had become so damn ineffective.

"He's gorgeous."

Ellie suppressed a grin and tried to keep her gaze glued to her date. Hard to do, of course, when Luke sat across the room, looking like he was about to pull a Rocky Balboa and start pounding someone. Exactly the reaction she'd hoped for. Jealousy was a powerful emotion and she was banking on it to help her plight. She needed Luke so consumed with jealousy that he acted on his attraction. Of course, acting on it would scare the crap out of him, he'd panic, throw in a quick *you're Josh's sister*, and leave town. Hopefully.

"Yeah, I guess he's gorgeous," she agreed. Grudgingly. "If you like the cranky type."

"Oh, I like." Miguel leaned forward and clasped her hand with his. He stroked her fingers and offered a seductive grin. "I could just eat him up."

She laughed, eyes twinkling with mischief. "What about Ricardo?"

Ah, Ricardo. Miguel had gushed so much about his significant other during the car ride over that Ellie felt as if she knew everything there was to know about Ricardo Diaz. He was twenty-nine, worked on a factory assembly line, was apparently drop-dead gorgeous, and Miguel was absolutely crazy about him. Ellie's date had spoken about his boyfriend with such passion and adoration that she'd felt a pang of envy.

When was the last time she'd felt that way about another person?

"Ricardo and I have an agreement. We're allowed to window-shop. Going into the store is another matter." Miguel chuckled. "But trust me, if I wasn't taken, I'd buy out your friend's store."

Ellie rolled her eyes and then snuck a look in Luke's direction. She turned her head before their gazes could meet, but his furious expression had been unmistakable. When she glanced back at Miguel, he was watching her knowingly.

"You totally want this guy, don't you?"

She sighed. "It's that obvious?"

"Yes."

Her sigh turned into a low groan. "I always had a crush on him, you know? But he constantly treated me like a kid. He still treats me that way now. He thinks he can snap his fingers and I'll get on a plane like an obedient child."

"He's your brother's best friend, right?" When she nodded Miguel shrugged. "So tell your brother to call the guy off."

A burst of laughter shot out of her mouth. "My brother is the one who sent him."

Miguel paused. "Oh. Then tell bro to back off."

"Have you ever tried arguing with a lawyer?" She was about to say more when the back of her neck suddenly began to throb. Heat penetrated into her skin, as if someone had placed a heater at full blast behind her. Suppressing a groan, she turned her head again and found Luke glaring at her from across the room. How did he do that, manage to warm her skin even from ten feet away?

"Is your friend going to stare at us like that all night?" Miguel's voice contained a twinge of amusement.

"Probably."

"Then let's give him something to really get grumpy about." Miguel wiggled his dark brows and shot an impish smile in her direction. "Would you like to dance?"

Josh watched as Vivian replaced the cordless phone in its cradle and reached up to tuck a strand of blonde hair behind her ear. She shot him a smile and his cock hardened. Damn it, how did she do that? He'd been with many women, but he couldn't remember the last time he'd gotten so aroused from just one smile.

"Your sister is just fine," Vivian announced, tossing her

hair over her slender shoulders. She crossed the living room with sexy little strides and sank onto the armchair across from his. "And I want you to know, that's the last time I'll check up on her for you."

Check up on who? Oh, right, Ellie. Josh was suddenly distracted as he watched Viv lift a hand to her ear. She twirled the little gold hoop earring she wore, worrying her luscious bottom lip with her teeth at the same time.

She looked as preoccupied as he felt, and he knew why. It was that damn sexual tension. That loud crackling static that hissed through the air, growing louder the moment their eyes met. He wanted Vivian. He wanted to kiss her and touch her and fuck her all night long. And he knew she wanted it too.

He also knew she wouldn't admit it.

He'd spent the entire afternoon and evening in Viv's spacious home. Alone. About five seconds after she'd agreed to let him stay, Vivian announced she needed to do some shopping and whisked out the door. She'd been gone for four hours, during which he'd unpacked the small suitcase he'd brought and proceeded to do fifty push-ups. He hoped the workout would ease the tension in his body, but it hadn't. Instead, he'd thought only of Vivian, how incredible she looked, and how much he wanted sleep with her.

He hated that nonchalant way she looked at him, as if the electricity between them was one-sided. He hated the way she'd barely spoken to him since returning from the market, and the way she made sure to stand or sit at least three feet away from him, as if she was scared of what he might do.

Or maybe what *she* might do.

"Josh? Are you listening?"

He lifted his head and saw her gaze on him. She had spectacular eyes. Dark forest green, with flecks of yellow around her pupils. Like a cat. "Sorry, what?"

"I said, Ellie is at my club with a friend. Luke, apparently, is there too. According to my bartender, he's watching her like a hawk."

"Good," Josh muttered absently.

At the moment his mind was not on Ellie or Luke. It was focused solely on the gorgeous blonde sitting in front of him. He'd spent too many sleepless nights thinking about her. Vivian stirred a passion in him like no other woman ever had, but it was more than that. They had a connection. She understood him, and he thought he understood her. The age difference between them didn't matter. Not to him at least.

"Does it matter to you?" The words slid out of his mouth before he could stop them, and he knew from the way Vivian furrowed her delicate blonde eyebrows that he'd confused her.

"Does what matter?"

"My age."

Those two words hung in the air for what seemed like an eternity. Looking at the expression on Viv's face, he knew the answer. A twinge of sadness shone in her eyes, mingled with regret to create a look that plainly said yes.

"It shouldn't matter," he said before she could voice her reply. "We're both adults."

Vivian still didn't say a word, so he got up and closed the distance between them. He dropped to his knees and placed both hands on her lap, almost groaning at the feel of her shapely thighs under his palms. Damn, she was all curves. All woman.

"Josh...don't." Her whispered plea didn't stop him from caressing her thighs. Running his hands over the silky material of the skirt she wore.

"We're attracted to each other, Viv. There's no point in fighting it."

He felt her shiver under his touch and it prompted him to slide one hand lower, to the hem of her skirt. He grazed the pad of his thumb over the bare skin of her knee. Relished in its smoothness. Then he slid his fingers under her skirt and stroked her inner thighs.

"This can never go anywhere," she murmured, anguish and arousal mixing together in her throaty voice. "I'm too old for you. I have a grown daughter."

"And I have a grown sister who I raised by myself," he returned. "So what? Like I said, we're both adults."

"You should be thinking about settling down and getting married. Having kids. You won't have that with me."

"Says who?" he taunted, teasing her smooth hot skin with feather-light caresses.

"It won't work. *We* don't work."

"I disagree." He ran his fingers over the crotch of her panties. Felt the dampness there. Heard her soft whimper. And almost came in his slacks.

"Josh, please."

"Please what? Stop or go on?" He palmed her pussy, wanting so badly to tear her panties off.

Her response was a muffled "stop", followed by a soft moan.

He gave a faint chuckle. "I don't think what you say and what you want is the same thing, honey." He maneuvered one finger to the edge of her silky underwear and searched her flushed face. "You sure you want me to stop?"

"Yes." Her strangled answer was betrayed by the trembling of her thighs.

If her reaction to his touch wasn't so damn obvious he

would've put an end to his slow torture, but fortunately her desire was unmistakable. Her green eyes simmered with passion, her nipples clearly protruded against her thin cotton tank top and her clit throbbed and swelled under his hand. She wanted him. They both knew it. He just wished she'd stop fighting it and give in.

"I want you to look me in the eye and tell me you don't like what I'm doing."

She opened her mouth. "I don't—" She halted as he dipped a finger inside her panties and slid it over her slick folds.

She moaned again. Loudly. Without inhibition. The sound sent pulses of heat through him, causing his mouth to ache with the need to kiss her and his cock to throb with the need to be inside her. But still he held back, waiting, clinging to every morsel of control he had left.

"Still want me to stop?" he asked, surprised by the steadiness of his voice.

Her slender throat bobbed as she swallowed. Her eyelids fluttered, her chest rose and fell with each breath she took. He continued to wait, his hand motionless over her mound, fingers tingling with anticipation.

"No," she finally cried out.

He applied pressure on her swollen clit. "No what?"

"I don't want you to stop. I want..." She struggled for breath. "I want..."

He didn't give her the chance to finish. He released a savage groan from his throat at the same time as he pushed her skirt up to her waist. Her wetness covered his finger, driving him wild with desire, but he restrained himself. Shucking his khakis and thrusting into her wet heat would be damn easy, but he didn't want to do that. Yet. First he wanted to show Vivian Kendrick exactly what he had to offer.

An unbearable silence filled the room as he pulled her panties down her legs and tossed them on the hardwood floor. He wanted her to say his name, wanted her to cry out her arousal, but she didn't. So he did the only thing he knew would cause her to lose control. He lowered his face between her thighs and slid his tongue over her clit.

Vivian let out a sexy cry that would've made any man proud. Her pleasure filled him, fueled him, drove him to devour and explore her body with fervor. He kissed. Nibbled. Licked. Sucked. Swirled his tongue over her hot folds and pushed two fingers into her pussy until he felt her climax rip through her in shaky shudders.

Never in his life had Josh achieved such satisfaction from bringing a woman to orgasm. His erection was harder than granite, straining against his boxers and pleading for release. *Not yet.*

He kissed her one last time before raising himself up so that his face was inches from hers. Christ, he'd never seen a sexier sight. Viv's cheeks flushed in a way that made her appear almost girlish, and those ragged breaths that burst from her delicate throat made him mad with lust.

He wanted to express his need for her but all that came out was a strangled, "Vivian." Then he covered her lips with his, his mouth becoming a magnet that refused to pull away. He kissed her. Over and over again. Thrust his tongue in her mouth and shoved a hand in her hair.

He didn't know how long they remained there, kissing. Him on his knees with a rock-hard erection. Her on the chair, skirt pulled up, her sweet mouth exploring his with urgency.

"Viv." He pulled back and swallowed, moistening the throat that had grown dry and tight with need. "I want—"

And then the phone rang.

As if she were emerging from a hazy dream, Viv's eyes snapped open. Her hands fell from his shoulders. Her mouth closed.

"Don't answer it." His eyes pleaded with her but it was already too late. He saw the remorseful look on her face and knew she'd slipped out of his grasp yet again. Whatever they'd just shared ceased. She was in control again.

"Josh." Her voice was timid.

A spurt of anger bubbled in his gut. "Don't say it," he warned. "Don't say this was another mistake."

Their gazes locked, his glinting with determination, hers expressionless. Then she stood, gingerly moved around him and walked toward a nearby table. The mechanical ringing stopped as she clicked on the cordless phone and placed it to her ear. The "hello" she uttered was curt, but her tone softened a second later. "Tanya, hi! No, sweetie, I'm not busy at all."

Her voice sounded strained to Josh's ears but when she covered the mouthpiece with her hand and turned to him, she spoke calmly and quietly. "It's my daughter. I'll take the call in my bedroom."

As Josh watched her saunter away, his chest sagged. Inside him, a balloon of lust and anger, disappointment and hope, deflated as if someone had pricked it with a needle. It floated down to the pit of his stomach, coiling into a knot of pain.

The last thing he heard Vivian say before her bedroom door latched shut was, "No, honey, I was just talking to the pool boy."

CB

"I'd love to."

Luke instantly cocked his head the second he heard Ellie's voice break through the chatter of the club. Suspicion slammed into him like a gust of wind as he wondered what she'd just agreed to. No doubt something that would make him crazy.

Or turn him on.

Across the room, Ellie's date stood up and held out his arm. Luke clenched his fists as he saw her take the guy's hand and lead him to the jukebox. As they examined the song selections, Enrique's hand slid down Ellie's back to rest on the curve of her bottom.

Anger jolted through Luke like volts of electricity. He resisted every urge to run over there and slam his fist against the other man's clean-shaven jaw.

Clamping his fingers against the beer bottle, he tried to calm himself. Okay, some guy had his hands on Ellie's sweet ass. No big deal. It could be worse.

And a few moments later, Luke saw exactly how worse it could be.

As a sexy salsa number filled the room, Ellie and her date strolled onto the dance floor in front of the stage and began moving together in the most erotic dance Luke had ever witnessed.

Dear Lord, she knew how to move. As if her body was liquid, Ellie gyrated against her date. Hips swaying. Butt wiggling. Breasts...rubbing against the guy's chest.

Luke's mouth went dry, and against all his better sense he imagined Ellie moving like that against him. His body tightened with need, and at each wiggle of her hips against Enrique's groin, Luke's own groin clenched. When her date ran his hands up and down her back, her tailbone, her butt, it was Luke's fingers that sizzled.

A temptress, that's what she was. She moved with agility, confidence and a hell of a lot of sex appeal. Along with his unbearable desire came admiration. She was good at what she did. Born to be a dancer. Whether ballet, jazz or this intoxicating salsa tune, she belonged out on that dance floor.

As the sensual dance continued, an unwelcome pang of guilt gnawed at his gut. Ellie looked happy out there, and from what Josh had told him, she'd been miserable back in San Francisco. Absolutely miserable. Was it right to bring her back to a life of unhappiness? Could he really live with himself knowing he'd doomed her to that?

Taking a gulp of his beer, he debated getting out of here. Leaving, hopping on the next plane back to San Francisco and forgetting he'd ever bothered Ellie.

When she turned her head and met his gaze, he quickly changed his mind. Their eyes locked in a heated stare, and even if he'd tried, he wouldn't have been able to look away. Her big blue eyes flashed with...with that? She didn't look irritated to see him. She didn't look angry, either.

She looked pleased.

Her gaze flickered from him to her date, then back at him again. A small smile tugged at her full lips, and she continued to eye him, looking thoughtful, mischievous. And then, never once breaking their gaze, she ran her hands down Enrique's chest and proceeded to dance her way down his hips, until her face was inches from his crotch.

Luke shot to his feet.

Too far. Ellie knew she'd crossed the line the second Luke jumped from his chair and marched toward her and Miguel. Fire flashed in his gray eyes, filling the room—and her body— with a rush of heat.

She fought against the heavy thudding of her heart, gathering up confidence she didn't have and wishing she'd never decided to take this course of action.

"I need to talk to you." Luke's voice was rough, tinged with danger. He didn't once glance in the direction of Miguel. Didn't ask permission, just grabbed her arm and began leading her across the dance floor.

Her pulse quickened at the feel of his warm hand against her bare arm, but the brief desire-filled reaction dissolved into anger as he dragged her through the bar.

With a helpless glance over her shoulder, she silently pleaded with Miguel to step in, but her date looked too stunned by Luke's macho display to move.

"What do you think you're doing?" she hissed as Luke led her out the door of the club and into the humid night air.

He didn't speak, just tugged on her arm again and directed her to the alley next to the Dancehall. Darkness enveloped them, but the inferno still raging in Luke's eyes was enough to light up an entire city street.

"You're playing with fire," he hissed back.

Playing with fire. There it was, that phrase again.

She took a step back, her back against the brick wall, hoping to put some distance between them. Hoping her heartbeat would slow. But Luke only moved closer, until his denim-clad thighs pressed against hers.

"Don't think I don't know what you're doing." His hard gaze made her legs shake.

"I'm not doing anything." Her squeaky reply sounded unconvincing and they both knew it.

"Don't test me, Elenore. There's only so much a man can take."

81

Heat spilled through her cheeks. What was he saying, that he wanted her? No, that couldn't be true. He didn't want her, never had. Teasing him was supposed to make him head for the hills at top speed, not turn him on.

So why did he look turned on right now?

His silver-gray eyes continued to glimmer, with anger, heat. Lust. Dear God, lust. And as he stepped closer, pressed himself against her, Ellie felt the unmistakable hardness of his body.

"I'm on a date," she whispered.

"Bullshit. You're putting on a show." He chuckled, low and menacing. "For me."

The hard ridge of his erection brushed over her pelvis, and shockwaves singed each and every nerve ending in her body. A dull ache settled between her thighs. Her breasts grew heavy, her nipples hard. The dark alley seemed to grow even darker, until shadows danced over Luke's head, making him appear dangerous and seductive at the same time.

How had this happened? How had she gone from the seductress to the seduced?

"Luke..." Her voiced trailed off, the sound of his name coming out in a breathy whisper.

"Don't Luke me." His eyes narrowed into two dark slits. "You came here tonight to get to me, Ellie."

"No." *Liar.*

He dug his fingers into her arm, eliciting a swarm of shivers in her skin. "You wanted to make me jealous. That's why you were rubbing yourself all over that guy. Isn't that right?"

She swallowed hard before finding her voice. "Is there a reason you'd be jealous?"

Uncertainty flashed in his eyes, and the brief show of weakness gave her the confidence to continue.

"I'm Josh's little sister, remember? Nothing more. So why would you be jealous? Why would the sight of me rubbing against another man make you this crazy?"

His body tensed. "You're playing games with me, Ellie."

She held his gaze. His face hovered over hers.

"And I can tell you right now exactly how this game will end," he added, his voice rough.

"How?" God, why had she asked? She didn't want to know the answer at all.

He let out a harsh laugh. "You're a fool if you don't know that."

"Luke—"

He slammed his mouth on hers and parted her lips with his tongue without invitation.

Oh God. His mouth felt and tasted like heaven. With the skilled ease of a man who'd obviously kissed many women in his time, his tongue explored her mouth, hot and greedy.

He demanded and all she could do was give. The sharp, urgent thrusts of his tongue, as it swirled and pushed against hers, were almost too much to bear. Heat spiraled down her body, hardening her nipples, making her clit swell. When he shoved a knee in between her thighs and pressed his straining erection against her, it was all she could do not to sink to the pavement.

Against all common sense, she reached up and held onto his shoulders, steadying herself, searching for the strength to put an end to this explosive, body-numbing kiss. But she couldn't. As one of his hands tangled in her hair, angling her head to give him better access to her mouth, she simply whimpered. When his other hand cupped her breast over the thin fabric of her dress, the whimper became a moan.

The sound reverberated against their mouths, sending a tornado of shivers spinning through her body, until she could barely let out a breath. Her breast throbbed under his touch, and a desperate wave of hunger crashed over her. She wanted his hands and mouth on her. All over her.

Pulling back, Luke's lips hovered over hers. "This is what happens when you play games with me," he muttered, keeping his hand firmly on her breast.

Wordlessly, she met his gaze, shocked by the need and urgency she saw in those gray eyes. "Luke—"

He didn't let her finish, just covered her mouth with his, and gave her another toe-curling and knee-buckling kiss, before prying his lips away and taking a step back.

His eyes glimmered with desire. Anger. Satisfaction. He looked pleased with himself, like he believed he'd won this round. And truth was, he had.

"Remember this." His voice was low, tinged with danger. "Because the next time you flaunt yourself in order to get to me, it won't end with just one kiss. And believe me, I won't be as gentle."

Ellie forced her mouth closed. Gentle? What on earth was his definition of gentle? The way her body still ached from his erotic assault, she wondered, what did he consider *rough*?

And a better question—did she even want to know?

Chapter Six

"It's time for Plan B," Ellie announced the next morning. She turned to Vivian with a look of steel in her eyes.

"What's Plan B?" Vivian asked, her expression distant as she stirred the iced-latte in front of her with a plastic straw.

Well, this was odd. Ellie had never seen her boss look as distracted as she did now. Vivian was the epitome of cool, calm and collected. Always alert, always ready with a sharp comeback. Not today, though. Ellie had a feeling she could declare aliens had landed in her backyard and demanded she board their ship and Vivian wouldn't even blink.

But Ellie definitely understood distraction. Her head had been all over the place since the moment she'd opened her eyes this morning. Not only that, but she'd had to take a cold shower. A *cold shower*. It was seriously sad that twenty-four hours after Luke's kiss she still needed to cool the desire raging her body. Even sadder that the shower hadn't helped at all.

She'd hoped going into town with Vivian might help her organize her thoughts and regain focus. So far it hadn't.

They were seated in the outdoor patio of a little Mexican restaurant Ellie loved. Overhead, the sun dominated the clear blue sky, its heat sweeping through the main tourist strip of San Valdez in the form of a balmy breeze. Most of the shop owners had rolled out racks of merchandise onto the uneven sidewalk and were beckoning the occasional August tourist to stop by and examine their grossly overpriced goods.

Normally Ellie got a kick out of seeing the pale-skinned, Hawaiian-shirt-clad people barter with the shop owners. This morning, though, her sense of humor eluded her.

"Subtle isn't going to cut it anymore," she declared, then lifted her glass to her lips and took a sip of ice water. She slammed the cup down on the stained wood table, causing the ice cubes to whirl around and collide into each other.

"Okay," Vivian said, finally snapping out of whatever funk she was in.

"I need to bring out the big guns. Throw all my cards on the table." She pursed her lips together in thought. "I'm going to tell Luke I want to sleep with him."

Vivian raised her eyebrows. "Really?"

"Yep. I think it's the only way I can get him to leave."

But do you want him to leave?

The little voice in her head was seriously annoying her today. Of course she wanted him to leave. Unless she agreed to come home, Luke would continue to hang around and pressure her, and she was sick of being pressured. So what if his hot mouth had felt wonderful against hers? So what if her lips still tingled from his kiss?

"Where is all this coming from?" Vivian paused. "What exactly happened last night?"

Ellie suppressed a groan. "Luke happened."

Vivian's face lit up for the first time all day. "Ah, so the plan worked. Seeing you with Miguel succeeded in making him jealous."

"Oh yeah." She blew out a sharp breath. "He kissed me."

Kissed her? Wasn't that the understatement of the year.

More like he'd greedily *devoured* her.

"I see. Well, did you like it?"

She moaned. "Yes." Not only had she enjoyed it, but the second Luke's lips had crushed over hers she'd felt as though it had been meant to be.

She'd pined over the guy for so long it was almost ridiculous. He'd been her first crush. The star of her early sexual fantasies. The guy she'd wanted to lose her virginity to. God, how incredible would it have been if Luke was her first. But he hadn't been, of course. Scott had. Sometimes she still wished she'd acted differently, never gotten involved with Scott, waited for the right man.

But how was she supposed to know Scott would throw her away like a piece of garbage after—

Don't think about it.

"What's wrong?"

The urgency in Vivian's voice snapped Ellie out of her thoughts. She found her boss's green-eyed gaze searching her face with concern.

"Nothing's wrong," she said quickly.

"Then why do you look like you're about to cry?"

"I...I'm fine." She took a breath. "I was just thinking about...the past. That's all."

Vivian reached a manicured hand across the table, grasped Ellie's hand with it and held it tightly. "You're white as a ghost, honey."

She turned to the front window of the restaurant to examine her reflection and was surprised to see she did look a bit pale. Thinking about Scott always did that to her, made her feel weak and dizzy.

She let out a shaky breath and struggled to find words that

87

would ease Viv's worry. "When Luke kissed me...it just made me wonder what it would be like, you know, to actually *be* with Luke."

"You may not have to wonder anymore."

"What?" she asked.

"Well, if he kissed you last night, maybe he's starting to see you as more than his friend's sister."

Maybe there was some truth to that. Ellie remembered the way he'd pressed against her, his unmistakable erection. There was no doubt in her mind he'd been turned on. That *she'd* turned him on. But with Luke, even the obvious wasn't as obvious as it seemed to be.

Although they'd known each other for fifteen years, she had no clue what was in his heart. All of his relationships were brief, fleeting, you blinked and he had another woman on his arm. And that had always made her wonder.

She knew his childhood hadn't been traumatic. His parents had been happily married until his mother died when he was a teenager. His father seemed like a kind, down-to-earth man, at least from the few times Ellie had met him. And as far as she knew, Luke hadn't been in any disastrous relationships that might have scarred him for all other women. So why was he still a bachelor? Did he simply like the casual lifestyle, or was there something more to it?

And why did it matter? There was no point in analyzing Luke's love life, especially when she would never be a part of it.

"Maybe he is seeing me as something more," she relented, glancing at her boss. "But even if that's so, it doesn't mean anything. Luke and I will never have a relationship."

"Why not?" Vivian shrugged. "You two are both young, single, annoyingly stubborn. If you ask me, you're the perfect match."

She swallowed the lump in the back of her throat. "I don't have anything to offer a man, Viv. Not anymore."

Her friend's eyes narrowed, sharp as a hawk, but there was also sympathy in that gaze. "Ellie, what happened after the car accident? You've been hinting at something since the day you came here, and for the life of me, I can't figure it out." Vivian exhaled slowly. "What really happened with Scott?"

Ellie's throat went dry. God, she couldn't count the number of times she'd been asked that by her brother. Like if she opened her mouth and revealed the truth he could make it better.

Yet as she looked at Vivian, saw the softness in her eyes, she couldn't lie anymore. For so long, it felt like a weight was pressing down on her body, the cold revelation that refused to go away. She hadn't talked about it with anyone, and carrying the solitary burden was becoming too much. Just this time she wanted to ease the load, have someone else bear that burden with her.

Inhaling the warm salty breeze, Ellie gave in. "There were complications after the accident."

Vivian's gaze offered encouragement. "What kind of complications?"

"The miscarriage." She bit her lower lip. "After I lost the baby, the doctors told me I couldn't have any more children."

A short silence descended, until Vivian broke it with, "Are you sure? I mean—"

"I had an emergency hysterectomy, Viv."

The confession hung in the air, making it difficult to breathe. Her lungs heaved, desperate for oxygen, but the air was laced with a bitter taste that choked Ellie's throat. She'd said it. After months of bottling it up inside, she'd said it out loud.

"That's why Scott left me," she continued, surprised by how steady her voice sounded. "He said he refused to be with a woman who couldn't offer him children." She sucked in a breath. "He said I was damaged."

"Excuse me? Are you serious?" When Ellie nodded, Vivian let out a curse. "Well, then he's insane. Not only insane, but disgustingly insensitive. In fact, the only thing he is, pardon my French, is a complete asshole." Shock and anger glittered in her eyes. "Don't you ever believe that."

The fury in Vivian's voice touched her. After the accident, she'd been angry too. Her rage and indignation had helped her get through those first couple of weeks, but when the reality of the situation sunk in, shame and sorrow had replaced her volatile emotions. Her career was over, her fiancé had left her, her baby was gone, and as time passed she'd begun to wonder. If her own fiancé couldn't handle her situation, what other man would?

"I don't believe it," she said quietly. "Most of the time, anyway."

"Most of the time?" Vivian echoed. "Oh no, hon, there is no truth whatsoever in what that man said to you. You're a gorgeous, intelligent, *desirable* woman. The fact that Luke is panting after you proves that."

Ellie had to admit Viv's words were an echo of her own thoughts. Last night, in Luke's passionate embrace, she'd felt more like a woman than ever. The way his strong hands had cupped her breasts, the way his erection had pushed against her sex. Luke had made her feel something she hadn't in a long time. Wanted.

It would be so easy to fall into bed with him. If she pushed him hard enough, he'd give in sooner or later. He'd probably be an amazing lover too. But she also knew if she slept with him, she'd be risking her heart. She'd been half in love with him all her life. She didn't think she could handle being just another notch on his belt.

"It does feel nice knowing Luke is attracted to me." She slugged back the rest of her water and pushed the glass away. "But it would be nicer if he was here because he wanted to be and not because Josh forced him to—"

Before she could finish her sentence, Vivian broke out in a fit of coughs. She reached for her iced-coffee and took a long sip, then flashed an apologetic glance. "My throat. It got dry all of a sudden."

The explanation was as flimsy as they came, but for the life of her, Ellie couldn't figure out what she'd said to make Viv look this nervous. She didn't get the chance to question her, either, as Vivian cleared her throat and said, "So, ready to get out of here?"

Ellie nodded, and the two women dropped a few bills on the table to pay for their drinks then left the little patio. They had driven to town in Vivian's bright yellow Jeep, parked it on the outskirts of the downtown core and opted to stroll the strip. Neither woman said much as they walked down the sidewalk, dodging passersby and firmly shaking their heads at the merchants who tried to pull them over.

They were halfway to the car when Ellie stopped in her tracks. "Oh my God! It's perfect."

She stared at the display window of San Valdez's only decent clothing store, mesmerized. Vivian came up beside her, took one look at the mannequin and chuckled. "Luke will faint if you ever wear that around him."

"That's the plan." Without another word, Ellie strode into the boutique and made a beeline for the cash counter. The plump, dark-haired saleswoman standing there barely had time to say hello as Ellie pointed to the dress and said, "I want that one."

The woman followed Ellie's finger and smiled knowingly. "Oh yes. Wonderful selection." She had a heavy Spanish accent. "You are size five, six, yes?"

"Six."

"I will get you dress in this size." The woman scurried past a curtain that led into a back room. She returned seconds later with the dress and handed it to Ellie.

With a small grin, Ellie ran her fingers over the red satin then held the garment over the T-shirt and denim shorts she wore. The silky material just barely reached her lower thighs and the neckline plunged so low she knew Luke's eyes would pop out when he saw her in the dress. Which is why she had to have it.

"How much is it?" she asked the saleslady.

"One hundred and twenty."

The price was steep, but worth it. Grin widening, Ellie reached into her purse and pulled out her wallet. "I'll take it."

Moments later, her bank card was being swiped through the outdated machine and Ellie was punching in her PIN. She looked over at Vivian as she waited for a receipt, unable to contain her glee. "So here's the plan," she said. "I'll ask Luke out tonight, wear this dress and—"

"There is problem with card." The sales lady cut her off, smiling apologetically.

"What kind of problem?" Ellie asked in surprise.

The woman handed her a slip that said "Transaction Declined. Exceeded daily limit". She furrowed her brows as she read the cryptic words. "Limit? I don't have a limit."

"Maybe it's the machine," Vivian suggested. "There's an

ATM around the corner. You could try withdrawing cash."

Ellie told the woman to hold the dress for her, then left the store. Her sandals clicked against the cracked pavement as she headed for the machine, with Vivian struggling to keep up. "I don't get it," she muttered to herself.

She went through the motions of sliding her card into the ATM, punching in her PIN and the amount she wanted to withdraw, and waited.

"What the hell!" She cursed as the machine spat out a slip of paper that again told her she'd exceeded her limit. Confusion muddled her brain as she stared at it. "This makes no sense," she finally said, turning to Viv. "The only time I've had a limit on my withdrawals was in college. Josh set up the account for me but when I graduated we changed it to..." She suddenly growled. "That little—"

"Come on, honey, I doubt your brother would stoop so low," Vivian interjected.

"Are you kidding? This is exactly his style!" Ellie noticed her friend's cheeks had turned a rosy pink. She narrowed her eyes. "Are you getting heatstroke or something?" She didn't let Vivian answer, just changed the subject back to her slimy brother. "He thinks if he screws around with my bank account I'll come crawling home to him. Ha! Does he think I'm so dependent on him that I can't pick up the phone and call my own bank to undo what he did?"

"Ellie—"

She tightened her lips in a line of fury. "Well, he can think again."

"Ellie—"

"Vivian, I need to borrow one hundred and twenty dollars. Then I would like a ride home so I can call the bank. And once I finish doing that, I'm going to call Joshua Dawson and give him a piece of my mind."

"You froze her account?" Vivian slammed the front door behind her and stormed into the living room, where she found Josh wearing nothing but bright red swim trunks that sat low on his lean hips. Droplets from his dark hair fell onto his bare chest, sliding down his wiry chest hairs in rivulets. He'd obviously just come in from a swim and he looked good enough to eat.

Good thing Vivian wasn't hungry. She was furious.

"I didn't freeze her account." Josh shrugged, then reached for the fluffy blue towel sitting on the armchair and began dabbing his torso with it. "I merely called the bank and requested a daily limit of ten dollars be implemented."

He looked so smug Vivian wanted to strangle him. "What gave you the right?" she demanded.

"Ellie and I opened the account together. She apparently forgot to remove my name from it, which gives me the right to do anything I please."

"You're an asshole." The vicious words flew out of her mouth before she could stop them and the verbal attack left her feeling stunned.

What was she actually angry about? Did her rage come from her defense of Ellie or was she really just pissed off at herself for letting Josh get to her last night?

Still want me to stop? His low taunting voice floated into her head as a reminder that she'd had every opportunity not to let things get as far as they had. Stop. All she'd had to say was one little word and nothing would have happened. But had she done that? No, of course not. And now she was forced to deal with the consequences of her own stupidity.

God, she didn't want him here anymore. Though he was staying in the guest room at the end of the hall from her bedroom, it still wasn't far enough. Last night she'd lain awake, wanting so desperately to go to him, to slide into bed next to him and let him finish what he'd started in the living room. She hadn't given in to temptation, though. Instead she'd spent the night tossing and turning, unsettled by the thought of Josh in her home, frightened of the way he made her feel and upset with herself for letting herself feel it.

What had come over her? She'd had no control yesterday, no willpower. Instead of pushing Josh away, she'd allowed him to get closer. She was forty-four years old, for Pete's sake. She knew the difference between love and lust. Knew the price of getting involved with the wrong man. The last time she'd done it, she wound up pregnant and alone. This time, however, she wasn't worried about herself. It was Josh she was concerned about.

He didn't get it. He deserved to be with a nice young woman who could give him a minivan full of children. Not her, not a woman who was pushing fifty, a woman whose body was past its prime, a woman with a grown daughter who was practically his age. A woman he'd no doubt grow tired of.

She wasn't beating up on herself. She knew she had a lot to offer—to an older man. A man who would be satisfied with a casual affair.

Josh Dawson wasn't that man.

"I'm an asshole?" he echoed. His lips twisted in a bitter grimace. "I thought I was just the *pool boy*."

She fought back a rush of guilt. "You expected me to tell my daughter I was with her best friend's brother?"

"Yes." Josh's nostrils flared. "But I didn't realize what a

coward you were."

"A coward?" She shook her head, suddenly wanting to laugh out loud. "See, Josh, this is exactly why we can't be together. You're a kid. Impulsive, immature, throwing out insults when you don't get your way. A *child*."

Vivian instantly regretted her words as Josh's face turned red with anger and disbelief. Not to mention the flash of pain that was getting oh-too-familiar. She'd hurt him by saying that, but maybe that's what it would take for him to get the picture. To understand that the two of them were colossally wrong for each other.

She stood there quietly, watching various emotions dance in his blue eyes like colors in a kaleidoscope. Pain turned to irritation. Anger to bitterness. And finally a deep shade of determination.

"I'm a kid, huh?" He chuckled softly. "We'll see about that." Before she could reply to that cryptic remark, he spoke again. "Do you have access to the Internet on that thing?" He gestured to the computer sitting on the desk next to the kitchen doorway.

She nodded wordlessly.

"Good. Go boot up the computer while I make a call, will you, Viv?"

"So what exactly am I looking at?"

Josh watched as Vivian studied the photograph filling the computer screen. He'd asked his secretary to scan and email all the photos in the album he kept in his desk and, efficient as always, she'd sent the images in less than ten minutes. It had taken a few minutes to download everything, but now, as he stood behind Viv's chair and saw her wrinkle her nose, his confidence surged.

A child? He still couldn't believe she called him that, especially seeing as he'd stopped being a child at the age of fifteen. Immature was the most unsuitable adjective Viv could've picked to describe him. And he couldn't wait to show her just how wrong she was.

But first things first.

"I'll explain about the pictures in a minute," he replied. "First we make a deal."

She twisted in the chair to face him, green eyes wary. Why did she always have that expression on her face when she looked at him? As if it unsettled her just being near him.

"What kind of deal?" Suspicion lined her tone.

"I want to take you out on a date." He held up his hand before she could object. "After you hear me out, if you still think I'm a kid, fine, I won't push you anymore. I won't touch you or kiss you or so much as sneeze around you. But—" he smiled slightly "—if after seeing the pictures you change your mind about me being—what was it?—right, an impulsive, *immature* child, I reserve the right to take you out. Do we have a deal?"

He lifted his shoulders awaiting her answer. She didn't seem thrilled at the prospect of the two of them going out, but she didn't look repulsed, either.

After biting her bottom lip again, she finally sighed. "Fine. It's a deal."

"Good." He leaned forward and put his hand on the computer mouse, catching a whiff of Vivian's perfume as he bent. She didn't wear those fruity, flowery scents most females his age liked to douse themselves with. Viv's scent was more subtle, lemony, intoxicating, the kind of perfume a mature woman wore.

He inhaled deeply, branded the sexy smell into memory, and clicked on the first image. A pig-tailed nine-year-old Ellie beamed out at them, clad in a pink tutu and white ballet slippers. "This was Ellie's first major recital," he explained. "It fell on the same weekend my entire junior class went to Los Angeles for the year-end trip. I didn't go."

He moved to the next photo before Vivian could comment. "This is my high school graduation." He cringed at the out-of-focus shot of him accepting a diploma. "Don't mind the blurriness, Ellie's camera-challenged, but see all those students standing there with me?"

Vivian nodded. "Yeah."

"To this day I don't know any of their names. I graduated with them a year early instead of with my friends. I was sixteen."

"Josh, what's the point of all this?"

He moved the mouse. "Okay, me graduating from college, blurry again thanks to my sister. I was twenty." He paused. "You know I never went to a single party in college?"

"Why not?" she murmured, her face fixed on the monitor.

"I spent days attending classes and nights helping Ellie with her homework. Weekends I'd drive her to ballet." He chuckled. "I don't think my aunt even knew Ellie and I were living in her house. She was out day and night, doing God knows what. She was living off my uncle's life insurance, so she didn't have a job or any discernible responsibilities to take care of. She certainly didn't take care of us."

He absently skipped a few of the images, mostly Ellie at recitals, and clicked on one of himself and a pretty redhead. "Me and Cynthia, my first serious girlfriend. This was taken at a bed and breakfast we went to for one night while Ellie stayed at a friend's."

"You look exhausted." Vivian touched his face in the photograph and ran her index finger over the dark circles under his eyes.

"I was. I'd stayed up the night before cramming for the LSATs, then spent the morning taking Ellie to the dentist, ballet practice and then to her friend's house." He offered a wry grin that Vivian didn't see with her back turned to him. "Can you believe I fell asleep right in the middle of sex? Needless to say, Cynthia dumped me the next day."

Josh went through the pictures one by one, explaining each one calmly and with a little bit of self-deprecation. Damn, he really had led a boring life, hadn't he? Once he felt he'd hammered his point home, he logged off the Internet and switched off the computer, waiting for Vivian to say something.

When she didn't move, he firmly grasped the back of her chair and swiveled it around. "So?" he said, crossing his arms over his chest. He pinned her down with an expectant stare.

She stayed silent, making him want to reach out and shake her. Christ, hadn't those pictures been the proof she needed? To him, the images made everything pretty damn obvious. The moment his parents had died, any immaturity on his part had died with them. He'd spent his teenage years parenting his sister. He'd studied for law school instead of partying. He'd forsaken relationships so that he could build a stable career for himself, so that his little sister would be taken care of for the rest of her life. He'd never once dropped any of his burdens or responsibilities on someone else, and anyone who knew him now could argue that he was the oldest thirty-year-old on the goddamn planet.

So why the hell didn't Vivian Kendrick see it?

"I'm not a kid," he said, slightly startled by the menace in his tone. He quickly softened it. "I'm a man, sweetheart. I worked my ass off to become a lawyer, and like you, I spent most of my life taking care of someone else." His jaw tightened when Vivian still didn't answer. "If you can't see that, Viv, maybe I really am wasting my time."

He gave her a second to interject. Another second to object. Then he clenched his fists and swiftly turned away.

Her silence told him more than any words could say. She still thought he was a child. She still wouldn't let herself open her heart to him. He heard it loud and clear, despite the deafening quiet of the room.

Damn her.

Without glancing back, he strode down the hallway to the guest bedroom. His suitcase sat empty at the foot of the bed and he stared at it, knowing it was time to pack up and leave. What the hell else was he supposed to do? He'd given it his best shot, tried to make Vivian realize they were good for each other, but she didn't see it. No use sticking around and putting himself through any more misery.

His chest ached as he moved to the cedar dresser and began removing random items of clothing from the drawers. He was disappointed. He was angry. And he was saddened by the fact that the gorgeous blonde in the other room couldn't see what was right in front of her eyes.

Oh well. He'd get over her. He'd managed to function these last two years, succeeded in putting Viv and that goddamn kiss out of his mind and focused on his life. And he'd do it again. All he had to do now was talk some sense into his sister and then he'd be on the next plane out of this town.

"What are you doing?"

His fingers curled over a pair of socks in a tight fist. He saw Vivian in the doorway from the corner of his eye, but forced himself not to turn his head. Without acknowledging her, he continued grabbing items from the dresser and tossing them into the suitcase.

The sound of soft footsteps filled the room as Vivian slowly walked toward him. He froze again, feeling her come up beside him, smelling that damn scent of hers again. She lifted one hand and held onto his chin, pulling it toward her with two unyielding fingers. Unable to stop himself, he met her gaze.

"We had a deal," she said quietly.

He heard the trembling in her voice but didn't stop to analyze what it meant. Her hand felt too damn good on his face, her manicured fingertips brushing over his five o'clock shadow in a way that sent a single shiver tearing down his spine. What did she want from him? Why did she have to torture him like this?

"I'm keeping my end of that deal," he replied roughly. "I'm leaving."

He held back a groan as she slid her other hand up and cupped his face. "You said if I changed my mind about you that you'd take me out on a date." He saw her swallow. "Well, I changed my mind, Josh."

A small burst of hope swelled in his chest, making his heart beat a little faster and his breath come out a little sharper. "You did?"

She nodded, never breaking their gaze or letting go of his chin. For the first time since he'd gotten here she didn't appear wary. Right now she just looked calm and completely unruffled.

"I'm sorry for what I said," she added, lightly brushing her fingers over his lips. "You're right. There's nothing childish about you."

Well, hallelujah.

"And I would really like to go out with you." Her gorgeous lips curved in a tiny smile. "That is, if you still want me."

Chapter Seven

As Luke steered the SUV in the direction of Ellie's bungalow, he came to the conclusion that he was a complete fool. Not only had he kissed her senseless last night, but he'd actually warned her—*warned* her—that next time he would take it further.

Why the hell had he said that? The sleepless night he'd faced since walking Ellie back to the club and hightailing it out of there should've provided him with an answer, but it hadn't.

Kissing Ellie had been the stupidest thing he could have done, given the situation. He knew damn well what she'd been trying to do last night. She thought that if she pushed him hard enough, she'd scare him away. Under any other circumstances, her plan probably would've worked. But no matter how much she teased and taunted him, he knew he had to stay. Josh rarely asked for favors, and the fact that he'd trusted Luke to come after his sister was reason enough to stick around.

He wondered if Josh would still trust him if he knew what Luke had said to his sister last night.

Next time I won't be as gentle.

Christ, what was wrong with him?

With a groan, Luke pulled into the small driveway and killed the engine. His palms were unusually damp as he reached for the door handle. Damn, he had to talk to her about that kiss. If it were any other woman, he'd turn on the charm, explain it had been a mistake, and offer a quick *can we still be friends?* But it wasn't another woman. It was Elenore Dawson.

The image of her on the dance floor floated into his head, quickly followed by the memory of how soft her lips had felt under his and how warm her tongue had been as it swirled against his own. His cock instantly stirred, causing him to let out a string of expletives that fortunately nobody was around to hear. Why couldn't he turn off his desire?

Why do I have to?

The thought made him pause. He let go of the door handle and leaned back in the leather seat, staring out the windshield at Ellie's pink bungalow. Suddenly he was doubting himself. Hesitating. Reconsidering.

Why *couldn't* he get involved with Ellie? She was gorgeous, after all. Ridiculously stubborn, but he liked that about her. He also liked her fire. Her spunk. Her dancing amazed him. Her passion overwhelmed him. So what kept holding him back? Was it Josh, or was it simply—

The ringing of his cell phone interrupted his thoughts. Ironically, the second he glanced at the caller ID he remembered exactly why he couldn't be with Ellie.

"Hi, Dad," he said into the phone.

The sound of his father's voice brought on the usual feelings of pity and weariness, along with the sobering realization of why he'd decided to remain a bachelor all these years. It was a voice tinged with sorrow and pain, hopelessness and defeat.

"You'll be coming home next month, won't you, Lucas?" Gregory Russell sounded distressed.

"I'm not sure yet, Dad. I might be on assignment."

"But it's your mother's birthday."

My mother is dead. He wanted so badly to shout out those words but he bit them back. It was pointless. His father would probably never accept the fact that his wife was dead. She'd passed away from breast cancer almost a decade ago, yet the man still acted as if she was alive and kicking. He set the table for two every night when he ate dinner. He prepared two cups of coffee every morning when he woke up. He spoke of his wife in the present tense, kept all of her clothes hanging in their closet and bought her Christmas presents each year.

And he never forgot to celebrate her birthday. Gifts, cake, decorations, the whole production. Luke had humored his father at the beginning. He showed up for the birthday celebrations, casually ate his damn cake and acted like everything was normal. Until enough was finally enough.

He suspected that's why he'd been so drawn to bodyguard work. The constant traveling, never really getting too close to the people he was supposed to protect. Though he had a small apartment in San Francisco, he was very rarely there, and that suited him just fine. Living out of a suitcase sure as hell beat seeing his father on a daily basis, witnessing the old man's slow approach to the edge of insanity.

Luke did his best, though. Whenever he wasn't working he visited his dad. They had dinner together, watched the Super Bowl every year, even caught a Giants game once in a while. When they were out of the house, surrounded by people, Luke even forgot about his dad's deteriorating mental state. Until Gregory brought up Luke's mother—that's when the reality of the situation came rushing back.

Put him in a home. That had been Robin's solution, to sweep the problem under the rug and forget about it. But Luke would never have been able to live with himself if he'd just shipped his father off to an old-age home. His dad wasn't senile, he was just...off-kilter. And Luke simply didn't have the heart to send him away.

"I really hate to miss Mom's birthday," Luke said into the phone. He felt disgusted with himself for contributing to his father's delusions but he'd been doing it for so long it came naturally now.

"Well, you know we'd love to see you, but if you have to work..." Gregory sighed. "There's always next year."

"Right next year." Luke's chest began to ache and so he quickly ended the call. With an abrupt goodbye and the promise he'd call soon, he hung up the phone and let out a ragged breath.

With a sudden burst of determination, he hopped out of the car and strode up the path leading to Ellie's door. He needed to convince her to come home. That's the only way he could put a stop to this ridiculous infatuation he'd suddenly developed for her. Once Ellie was in San Francisco, Josh would get off his back. He could take an assignment that required he trek off to some remote location and forget all about that explosive kiss he'd shared with Ellie.

Feeling like a man with a plan, he rapped his knuckles against the door and waited. No more playing around. *Time to show her who the boss is.*

When the door swung open, however, it became clear exactly who the boss was. Not him, that's for sure.

"Were you in on it?" she demanded, her blue eyes blazing.

"Huh?"

She either ignored his startled expression or was just completely oblivious to it. With a loud huff, she spun on her heel and stormed back inside, leaving him standing in the open doorway.

Okay. So Ellie was pissed, that much was evident. But what was she pissed about? Fuck if he knew.

Luke stifled a groan, stepped inside the house and headed down the hallway. He found Ellie waiting for him in the middle of the living room, her hands on her hips and a frown on her face. He wondered if she realized how sexy she looked when she was angry. Her cheeks all flushed. Eyes on fire. He grew hard just looking at her.

"Since Josh is conveniently not answering his cell phone, I'd like you to pass along a message," she said in a clipped tone.

Luke slung his hands in the belt loops of his jeans. "Okay."

"Tell him that his little games aren't going to work. I called the bank and changed my account information, so let him know his latest ploy failed."

Though Luke had no idea what she was talking about, it wasn't hard to figure it out. Josh had obviously tried to manipulate his sister again, and as usual, Ellie wasn't having it. It was a game they'd played for years.

"I'll pass it along," Luke replied in a mild tone.

"Good." Her eyes continued to smolder. "Now I want to know if you knew about any of this."

"If it helps, I still don't know what you're talking about. Scout's honor." He held up three fingers in a sign he was fairly certain didn't represent the Boy Scouts whatsoever.

Ellie broke out in a grin. "We both know you're no Boy Scout." She paused. "I just made some lemonade. I'll get you a glass."

Before he could blink she bounded into the kitchen. *What the hell?* He had no idea what to make of her swift exit or the way her anger had melted away like an ice cube in the sun. But he'd seen that little glint in her eyes, the one that said she was up to something, and with Ellie that *something* always proved to be a headache.

In less than a minute, she reentered the room with two cups of lemonade and motioned for him to join her outside. She wore a filmy pink skirt that hugged the curve of her ass and Luke couldn't help but admire the sway of her hips as she walked. He fought the urge to run after her, spin her around and kiss her again. Then he cursed himself for having that annoying urge and trailed after her.

Luke sat on the chair across from hers and reached for the lemonade. After taking a long sip and hoping the cold liquid might numb his groin, he took a breath and spoke. "I'm sorry about last night."

The look of surprise on her fair face unnerved him. "Why are you sorry?"

"Because I barged in on your date. Because I, uh, kissed you." Damn, why did his voice sound so hoarse?

That uncharacteristic knot of insecurity coiling in his gut made him push forward. He wasn't going to give her the chance to speak, the opportunity to convince him the kiss hadn't been a mistake or that maybe more could come of it. "I want you to come home with me. Today." He held up his hand before she could object. "I'm serious, Ellie. No more excuses. You're leaving."

"Forget it." The fire returned to her eyes, the heat of it searing right through his cotton T-shirt.

"Why the hell not?" His words resonated with the frustration he felt.

She lifted her glass to her lips and took a long swig, then slammed it on the table. "My reasons are private, Luke. All I can say is there's nothing for me back in San Francisco."

"That's bullshit and you know it. You brother is there, the

ballet company is there." He fought an impatient breath. "I get that you're still upset that Scott left you, but trust me, there'll be other men."

She ignored the last remark. Raked her fingers through her chocolate-brown hair in an act of sheer aggravation. "Why can't you just accept that I need time away? Why must you and Josh keep pushing me?"

He softened his tone. "Do you think I like pushing you? Do you think I like pressuring you, making you angry? Do you think I like—" He clenched his fists, refusing to vocalize his attraction. "Please, just help me out here. Come home."

Ellie knew an opportunity when she saw one. This was it, her chance to drop the mother of all ultimatums on Luke Russell. As much as she wanted to continue arguing with him, to tell him exactly where he and her brother could go with their demands, she had to play it cool.

Josh's little trick with the bank today proved that it was time to take control of her own life. She'd always be grateful to her brother for being there for her during her childhood. With their aunt off gallivanting around town and neglecting her sister's orphaned children, Josh had stepped in and assumed the role of parent and protector. He'd given her advice when she needed it, encouraged her to work hard at ballet, held her in his arms when she woke up late at night after a bad dream. But Ellie was all grown up now, and she didn't need Josh's protection. Or Luke's.

Especially Luke's. The longer he stuck around, the greater the risk that she'd fall head over heels for him. She couldn't let that happen, not when she knew a relationship would never be in the cards for the two of them.

It didn't help that he looked so damn good today. His dark

hair was tousled, as if he'd just rolled out of bed, though only the woman he'd rolled *into* bed with would know for sure if that's how his hair looked fresh from sleep. And the way his defined pectorals rippled against his navy-blue T-shirt and gorgeous gray eyes shone under the afternoon sun only deepened his sexiness. No, he was more than sexy. Far more than that.

He was unadulterated temptation.

"I think I know a way we can help each other," she finally answered.

Suspicion instantly flooded his face. "Oh really?"

She took a slow breath. Okay, she could do this. Just play the part of vixen. She was good at pretending. Every ballet she performed she'd had to play a part, become another person. This would be a snap.

Yeah, right.

"Last night when you kissed me..." She let her voice trail off in what she hoped was a breathy way. "It made me realize something."

Luke shifted in his chair. "What's that?"

"How much I want you."

Desire flashed across his face, followed by discomfort. His obvious reaction to her caused her confidence to soar.

She got up with as much sexy grace as she could muster and eased down on the chair directly next to his. She could swear she saw him squirm. *Good.*

"Ellie—" He managed a strangled warning that abruptly halted the second she lowered her hand and pressed it directly on his firm thigh.

"I know you want the same thing as I do." Her confidence grew as fast as the bulge in his pants. Oh my. She swallowed hard, trying to find her voice and control the rush of warmth spiraling through her. Then she slid her hand higher and placed her palm directly over his hard-on. "Don't bother denying it, Luke. I can feel it."

His erection jutted against her hand, sending a rush of pure longing to her bloodstream. She lifted her head and locked her gaze with his. He looked as aroused as she felt. Her confidence tripled.

"So here's what I'm thinking." She ran her hand up and down his shaft, biting back a moan when she felt it stiffen even more. "We both want something from each other."

"Yeah?" A visible pulse throbbed in his throat, telling her that Luke Russell was most certainly not as controlled as his steady voice suggested.

"Oh yeah. You want me to return to San Francisco. And I—" She grasped his erection and pulled it gently. He exhaled sharply. "I want something a little different. Do you know what I want, Luke?"

"What do you want, Ellie?" he choked out.

Suddenly the stifling heat in the air had nothing do with the rays of the sun. Suddenly everything around her turned into an aphrodisiac. The hot grains of sand beneath her bare feet. The wicker chair beneath her butt. The sound of the waves crashing against the shore. Luke.

She leaned closer so that her lips brushed his ear, and whispered, "I want you to fuck me."

She pulled back just in time to see raw lust swimming in his silvery eyes, a look he quickly concealed with a furious scowl. "Christ, Ellie, where'd you learn to talk like that?" She simply smiled. "You can't be serious," he growled in response.

"I'm dead serious." She stroked his erection again but this time he pushed her hand away.

Knocking the chair back, he stumbled to his feet. "Well, forget it," he shot out.

Ellie leaned back and crossed her legs, casting him an innocent look. "The offer's on the table, Lucas. I'll come home. In exchange, you..." She trailed off and raised her eyebrows suggestively.

"I'm not going to sleep with you," he replied flatly.

"Why not? It's obvious you want to." She gave a careless shrug and sent a pointed stare at his impressive hard-on.

Luke clenched his fists. "What I want is irrelevant. It doesn't change the fact that sleeping together is *not* a good idea."

She laughed. "I disagree. I think it's a phenomenal idea." She caught his agitated expression and decided it was time to close in for the kill. "Bottom line, Lucas, I won't come home unless you give me one night of hot, wild sex."

"I didn't realize you'd added blackmail to your book of tricks," he said sourly.

She shrugged again. "Take it or leave it. But know that I'm completely serious. Either you take me to bed, or you'll have to consider relocating to San Valdez, because trust me, I'm not leaving."

His eyes narrowed. "I don't have time for games."

She didn't back down. "This isn't a game."

"Goddamn it." He let out a sound that was a cross between a growl and a roar, and then stomped toward her. He stood there for a moment, loomed over her, watched her. A knowing glint lit up his eyes. "I get it. You want me to call your bluff, don't you?"

Damn, why did he have to be too smart for his own good? "Oh, this isn't a bluff," she lied, hoping he couldn't see through her. "One night is all I'm asking for. Then you'll get your way. If you don't agree, you might as well give up and go home. Without me."

"Why do I still think you're bluffing?" he shot back.

Ellie stifled a groan. He always had to be difficult to the end, didn't he? Straightening her shoulders she rose from the chair and took a step toward him. He took a step back.

"I want you," she told him, moving even closer. This time he didn't budge so she took advantage and pressed her body to his. She slid her hands up his hard chest and loosely twined them around his neck. The air began to sizzle, sending a sweeping rush of heat down her body.

There was something liberating about Luke's obvious reaction to her nearness. It made her feel bold and brazen, feminine and desirable. His excitement was hot and thick against her pelvis and she wondered what it would feel like sliding inside her. Like heaven, no doubt.

"I also know you want me," she continued, brushing her lips over the hard curve of his jaw.

He flinched and tried disentangling her arms from his shoulders, but she held on tight. Trapped him in her embrace. "C'mon, Luke, the way I see it, you come out the winner in all this." She nuzzled his neck and trailed open-mouth kisses on his warm skin, thoroughly enjoying his harsh intake of breath. "You'll get me back to San Francisco and at the same time you'll have a little fun in the sack. If that isn't an offer you can't refuse, what is?"

Before he could answer, she pressed her mouth to his in a soft kiss. Her eyelids fluttered but she didn't close them. She wanted to see Luke, wanted to savor every delicious detail. His slitted eyes. The pounding of his pulse beneath her hand. The way he slid his tongue out to graze her lower lip yet held back from thrusting it in her mouth.

He was fighting something inside himself. She knew it. And that only made her all the more determined to win this battle.

She dragged her lips away from his and smiled when his eyes flew open in obvious disappointment. "So is that a yes?"

"If I sleep with you, you'll come home?" he returned roughly.

"Yep."

His handsome features creased in the epitome of defeat. "Then okay. You've got yourself a deal, Elenore."

What the hell had he gotten himself into?

Luke peeled out of the driveway, cringing as the sound of screeching rubber rang out. Shit. Hopefully Ellie hadn't heard that. When he'd left her house, he'd let her believe he was perfectly okay with this latest development. He didn't want her thinking that...that what?

He was nervous?

He was terrified?

He was about to come in his pants from the anticipation?

His body tensed at the last thought. Damn it, why was he anticipating an event that would never even happen?

With his fingers curled over the steering wheel in a death grip, he drove twenty miles over the speed limit and tried to collect the willpower he'd thrown out the window the second Ellie kissed him. He drove aimlessly, not ready to return to the motel and be alone with his thoughts. No, right now he needed to strategize.

The streets of San Valdez were deserted as he maneuvered the SUV through them. He still found it strange that the town was located just a few hours from San Diego County, yet had a population of less than ten thousand. The absence of shopping malls and endless concrete lots unnerved him, made him feel as if he were driving through a ghost town. Which was probably a good thing at the moment, because he was so distracted he'd probably have mowed over dozens of pedestrians on his joyride.

Only when he reached a residential stretch of road did he slow the vehicle, but he still didn't release his grip on the wheel. He'd agreed to sleep with Ellie. Was he insane? Obviously.

You're not going to sleep with her, a little voice reminded him. *It's part of the game.*

"Did I mention how sick I am of games?" he muttered to his subconscious.

How had he let this situation get so out of control? His task had been simple—find Ellie, convince her to come home and let Josh deal with the rest. In his line of work he'd learned to keep a distance, to watch over the people he'd been hired to protect and leave when the job was over. The life of a bodyguard was rarely ever like the one portrayed in that movie with the same name. You didn't fall in love with your assignments, you didn't get too close, and you didn't let emotions interfere with your mission. Doing any of the above usually meant you got someone killed.

Not that there was any danger in the mission Josh had sent him on, unless you counted this ridiculous attraction to Ellie. But the same principles remained. Letting Ellie get under his skin would only slow him down. And turn him on.

He might have agreed to her preposterous ultimatum but he had no intention of taking her to bed. No matter how much his dick begged him to.

"She's bluffing," he mumbled to himself.

That's what he needed to hold on to, the knowledge that, like him, Ellie had no intention of following through on it. She

114

wanted to scare him. She thought she could use his basic male needs against him.

Well, Ellie wouldn't win this round. He'd play her little game, he'd *outplay* her, and in the end she would be the one to back down.

Not him.

"What the..." A flash of movement from the corner of his eye caught his attention and prompted him to slow the vehicle to the curb. He turned his head swiftly and found himself looking at a two-story, Spanish-style home with a green stucco roof. It wasn't the house that ensnared his gaze, but the couple leaving it.

He had to blink a few times to convince himself he wasn't hallucinating. He recognized Vivian instantly, as it was hard to miss a body that curvaceous and blonde hair that shiny. But was that Josh with her?

"You've gotta be kidding me," Luke muttered under his breath.

He watched as the couple across the street got into the bright yellow Jeep he'd seen parked behind the Dancehall. Vivian took the driver's seat and both she and her companion were oblivious to his parked SUV as the Jeep reversed out of the driveway. Luke kept his gaze glued to them, only looking away when the yellow vehicle took a left at the end of the street and disappeared.

Stunned, he loosened his grasp on the steering wheel to reach up and rake his fingers through his hair. A barrage of questions invaded his confused brain.

Josh was in town? Was he staying with Vivian? Why had they been looking at each other in that perplexing way?

And the most daunting question of all. What the hell was going on?

Chapter Eight

Later in the evening, Ellie got her usual ride to the club from Marlene, one of her fellow dancers. Making the fifteen-minute walk under the dusky night sky appealed to her as much as getting behind the wheel of a vehicle, but luckily Marlene lived nearby and had no problem with playing chauffeur four times a week. The two women were about the same age, though Marlene's bubbly personality and deep love of gossiping made her appear far younger. Because of Marlene, Ellie seemed to know the most trivial details about everyone in town, from the bartender at the Dancehall to the old Native American man who sold dream catchers in the market.

Tonight, though, she was startled to find Vivian the object of Marlene's chatter.

"So obviously *you* know who he is, right?" Marlene had one hand on the wheel of her beat-up red Honda. The other hand fumbled around in her large leopard-print purse.

Ellie cringed. "Both hands on the wheel, Marly." *Please.*

Marlene produced a pack of cigarettes and pulled one out, then tossed Ellie an amused grin. "You realize you tell me that every time we're in the car together? Don't worry, honey, I've never had an accident in all the years I've been driving."

The night's still young. Ellie pushed away the cold knot of fear pressing down on her chest and took a calming breath.

Marlene hadn't killed her yet, she reminded herself.

"I have no idea what you're talking about, by the way," Ellie said, hoping the change of subject would ease her nerves. "Viv would've mentioned if she was seeing someone."

Marlene's hand left the wheel again as she lit her cigarette with the car lighter. She exhaled deeply then blew a puff of smoke out the open window. "Trust me, my source is never wrong. He swears he saw Vivian and some guy earlier at El Delicioso," she said, naming a romantic restaurant on the outskirts of town.

Ellie rolled her eyes. "What source?"

"My cousin Paul. He works as a waiter there."

The answer made her pause. She'd met Marlene's cousin a few times when he'd come by the club, and she'd seen Vivian chatting with him on a couple occasions. If Paul said he saw Vivian at his place of work, he was probably telling the truth.

Ellie pursed her lips together in thought, realizing this actually made a little sense. Vivian seeing someone could explain her earlier behavior. Distracted, flushed, secretive—all signs that perhaps there *was* a new man in her life. But if so, why wouldn't she have told her?

"What did this guy look like?" she asked curiously.

Marlene let out another cloud of smoke before saying, "Tall, dark hair, oh, and Paul mentioned he looked younger than Viv."

Ellie narrowed her eyes. Tall, dark-haired and young? The description was about as vague as you could get and yet... Maybe she was crazy, but she had the strangest suspicion Marlene's cousin had seen Luke at that restaurant with Vivian.

She absently chewed the inside of her cheek and tried to erase the ridiculous idea forming in the back of her mind. Luke and Viv weren't—no, of course not. The two were most definitely *not* involved. If they'd been out together, it was for an entirely different reason. Talking about her maybe? Or...

Had Vivian joined forces with Luke to run her out of town?

"That's crazy," Ellie mumbled under her breath.

"What was that?" Marlene asked as she flicked her cigarette butt out the window. She turned into the parking lot of the club and slid into one of the gravel-covered spots.

"Huh? Oh nothing," Ellie replied, seeing the curious look on her friend's face. "I just, uh, find it hard to believe that Vivian wouldn't tell me she was dating someone."

Marlene lowered her voice. "Maybe he's married." She gave a conspiratorial grin.

"Maybe."

Ellie reached into the backseat for her garment bag and got out of the car, still distracted. She didn't know if Vivian was with Luke earlier, or what they were doing if they had been together, but one thing was for sure, she would definitely find out.

☙

Luke frowned to himself as he watched Ellie take her bows. The pathetic excuse for applause echoed through the club, mostly middle-aged men with leers on their faces who couldn't care less about the performance they'd just viewed. As long as they glimpsed a few flashes of skin and some tits bouncing around, they were happy to spend their weekly paychecks on beers and the small cover charge to get in to see the show.

Ellie deserved better than this. She deserved an entire auditorium filled to the max while bouquets of roses were thrown at her feet. A few years back Luke had seen her dance in *Swan Lake*, when he was guarding a socialite who spent her evenings at lavish parties and tasteful ballets and operas. He remembered the applause was deafening that night, a far cry from what he'd just heard.

Fortunately the show was finally over. Seeing Ellie in that corset again only reminded him of what he needed to do tonight. He was taking her to dinner once she finished changing and after that he thought he'd bring her to the carnival he kept seeing signs for around town. Dinner and a fair—it sounded so damn innocent, didn't it? Too bad it would be far from it.

Now that he'd had a few hours to think about it, he realized going along with Ellie's ultimatum was the best course of action. No way would she really go to bed with him. She simply wasn't that kind of girl. Now that he was thinking clearly, with his brain and not his cock, he was even more convinced that Ellie was yet again testing him. Trying to scare him. Well, he wasn't about to be scared off. Tonight he planned on teasing her, pushing her and letting her know exactly who was in control.

"Did you enjoy the show?"

He glanced up as Vivian slid into the seat across from him. In an instant, the memory of Vivian and Josh returned to his head, bringing with it a rush of suspicion. He studied Vivian's green eyes for a sign that she might've seen him driving past her house earlier, but he saw none. During his scrutiny, however, he couldn't help but admire her appearance. She really was a beautiful woman, her minimal makeup and silky golden hair giving her a child-like aura while her intelligent eyes revealed a maturity that couldn't be ignored.

He could understand why Josh would be attracted to her. If that were even true. At the moment Luke had no clue what Josh and Vivian had been doing together, though he certainly intended to find out.

"It was good," he replied, pushing away his half-empty beer. "Will Ellie be coming out soon?"

"She should be. It's a slow night, so I cancelled the second show, which means she's probably scrubbing the makeup off. She hates that stuff."

Luke kept his expression nonchalant. "Yeah, she's always hated it. I remember this one time, back when Josh and I were in college, he surprised Ellie with an entire case of makeup. Josh decided that since she was in high school she needed to look mature, but when he gave her the makeup she rolled her eyes and ever so politely said, 'I'm not a hooker, Joshua'."

He'd hoped mentioning Josh would rattle Vivian but all he got from her was a little laugh. "She's got a mouth on her, doesn't she?" Vivian said.

"Yes, she does." His jaw stiffened a little as he pondered the best way to approach the subject. He had two choices—either dance around the issue a bit longer and see if the woman said something, or just come right out and confront her.

In typical male fashion, he opted for instant gratification.

"I saw you this afternoon." He kept his tone light and leaned forward to rest his elbows on the table. Was that a spark of guilt in her eyes?

"You mean in town?" she returned smoothly, her composure quickly restored. "Yes, Ellie and I were shopping."

"No, it was after that. Around five or so. I was driving past your house." His lips curved in a little smile as he saw her face go a shade paler.

"Oh."

"How long has he been here?"

His question mingled in the air with the cigar smoke from

the man at the next table. The defiant look in Vivian's eyes made him think she would play dumb, but to his surprise she suddenly sighed and said, "Two days."

"He's staying at your place?" When she nodded, he added, "Does Ellie know?"

"He made me promise not to tell her." A defensive edge entered her voice. "He's not trying to interfere, he's just here to make sure his sister is okay."

Luke laughed. "Not interfere? That's what Josh is best at, sweetheart."

"Just don't tell Ellie he's here. She'll be furious. And, um, I'm working hard trying to convince him to go home."

He lifted his brows. "Are you?"

A slight pink flush rose in her cheeks. "Of course."

Luke didn't buy it. If he'd been doubtful before, he sure as hell wasn't now. There was something between Vivian and Josh. No question about it. Yet it didn't really surprise him. Josh had always been drawn to older women, maybe because the guy had never really gotten the chance to be a kid himself. What irked him was that Josh didn't trust him enough to handle Ellie on his own, that he'd had to take matters into his own hands and butt in.

Well, enough was enough. In one corner he had Josh breathing down his neck, requesting a favor and then charging in to do it himself. In the other he had Ellie teasing him with her sexy smiles and incredible body, asking him to fuck her and testing his control. And the situation would only get worse, unless Luke put a stop to it right now.

"You know what?" he finally said. "Why don't we just put all our cards on the table?"

Vivian swallowed, and then reached up to run her fingers

through her long blonde strands. "Meaning?"

He leaned closer, speaking quietly so that nobody would overhear. "I don't give a damn what's going on between you and Josh, but obviously you do or you wouldn't be keeping it a secret. All I want is for Ellie to leave this goddamn town and go home. That's all Josh wants too." He blew out a breath. "The way I see it, you're the only one who can make that happen."

A suspicious glint entered her eyes. "And how can I do that?"

"Ellie came here because of you. She has a job because of you." He set his mouth in a tight line. "I want you to fire her."

"Excuse me?"

"You heard me." His words were harsh but he didn't give a damn anymore. "Tonight I'm going to take Ellie out and show her I'm not playing her game anymore. And tomorrow when she comes in to work, you'll be informing her that she's fired."

The pink splotches on Vivian's cheeks darkened to a deep shade of crimson. She clasped her hands together tightly, the white on her knuckles telling him she was furious. "And I suppose if I don't agree, you'll tell Ellie that I lied to her about Josh being here?"

"I'm considering that, yes." He allowed his jaw to relax. "Look, Vivian, we both know Ellie doesn't belong here. She's hiding away from her life. She had to put her career on hold, her fiancé dumped her, and it hit her hard. Do you honestly believe her future is in this town?"

After a moment of silence, Vivian gave a grudging look and said, "No, I don't."

Luke's chest swelled with hope. "Then let her go. Don't give her a reason to stay." He reached across the table and gripped both her hands with his. "Fire her, Viv. You know it's for the best."

"I'll...think about it." She removed her hands from his grasp and shot him a knowing glance. "But just remember something, Luke. You're not Ellie's bodyguard. She doesn't need protection. She needs a friend."

Before he could question the cryptic remark, Vivian bounded from the chair and straightened the hem of her knee-length black skirt. With a small nod, she turned away and headed for the bar.

"What was that about?"

Luke jumped as Ellie's wary voice wafted from behind. A quick spurt of guilt erupted in his gut as he wondered just how much of the conversation she'd heard. Turning his head to explain, he opened his mouth, then closed it. His voice died in his throat.

Ellie looked...hot. So fucking hot it was practically criminal. She wore a short red dress that clung to every curve of her lithe body, from her small round breasts to her shapely thighs to that firm ass he still couldn't get over. Everything about the dress screamed *danger*. The treacherously low neckline. The ruby-red silk. The way it stopped just below her thighs and revealed long shapely legs and feet strapped in a pair of flat sandals. Christ, was she trying to kill him?

It took a second for him to snap out of it and move his gaze north, but what he saw there was just as enticing. Her long brown hair was loose, flowing down her shoulders in waves, and the makeup she'd worn during the performance was scrubbed off. Her face looked fresh and clean, save for the shiny pink lip gloss that had his mouth tingling. He wondered how those shimmering lips would feel wrapped around his cock.

"Are you going to answer the question?" she interrupted his inappropriate thoughts, frowning. "What were you and Viv talking about?"

"I was just telling Vivian where I plan on taking you tonight," he lied.

Her taut features relaxed. Slightly. "That's all?"

He ignored another burst of guilt, adding, "And then she warned me to take good care of you otherwise she'd kick my ass."

Ellie's face relaxed completely. "Oh. Sounds like Viv, all right." She paused. "So where *are* you taking me?"

"Dinner at your favorite—" he tried not to cringe, "—seafood restaurant. And then that carnival on the boardwalk. The owner of the motel told me it's a big thing around here."

Ellie rolled her eyes. "I wouldn't call a Ferris wheel and popcorn stand a big thing."

He stood up and slung his hands in the waistband of his faded jeans. "Do you want to go somewhere else?"

"No. I love carnivals, regardless of how crappy." She flashed a small grin that warmed his insides. "So, you ready to go?"

She took a step closer and the silky material of her dress swirled around her legs. Forcing himself not to ogle her again he nodded. "Let me just pay for my beer."

He dug into his back pocket and removed a five-dollar bill, then dropped it on the table and turned to Ellie. He spoke before he could stop himself. "Did I tell you how amazing you look in that dress?"

"You just did." She grinned again and this time it warmed more than his insides.

With his semi-hard cock straining against the fly of his jeans, he shot her a rueful look. "C'mon, let's get out of here."

CB

"Luke knows you're here." Vivian didn't give Josh a chance to reply as she flew through the front door and dropped her purse on the black end table near the couch. She'd forgotten her cell phone at home and, although she could've lived without it for a night, the conversation with Luke at the club had rattled her. So much that she'd felt the need to come home and talk to Josh about it.

It was almost comical, the amount of guilt currently weighing down her shoulders like a block of concrete. She was forty-four years old yet she felt like a disobedient schoolgirl who needed to be reprimanded by the headmaster. Lying to Ellie made her feel like slime. No, like a wad of chewing gum under someone's shoe.

How had she let Josh convince her to keep his presence a secret? She should've called Ellie the second he showed up on her doorstep. Instead, she'd allowed him to stay in her home and get under her skin. To take her on a date, for God's sake. And damn it, it had been a really good date.

They'd talked non-stop during dinner about everything from law to philosophy. There hadn't been a single awkward silence and she was almost ashamed to admit that Josh Dawson was more mature than most of the men she'd dated in the past. Maybe even more mature than her.

The evening had gone so well she'd had to fight the temptation to blow off work and spend more time with him. Of course, after her conversation with Luke Russell, she really wished she'd given in to that temptation and never gone to the club.

"You told him?" Josh said in surprise. He was sitting on her couch, flipping through a thick legal document. On the coffee table sat a stack of files he'd had his secretary FedEx to Vivian's house.

"He saw us," she corrected, sinking down next to Josh. "Apparently Luke was driving by as we were leaving for dinner."

Josh set the document on the table. "Oh."

"Oh? That's all you have to say? It doesn't bother you that Luke knows you're staying here...that we're, you know, together?"

"Why should it?" He shrugged then stretched out his arm and rested it over her shoulder. "Like I keep telling you, we're both adults. Who cares if Luke knows?"

An exasperated breath flew out of her mouth. "I care. Especially if he tells your sister that I lied to her. Which he won't, of course." She frowned. "Not if I do what he asked."

Josh returned the frown. "What the hell does that mean?"

"He wants me to fire Ellie so she won't have a reason to stay in town."

"I agree. Fire her, Viv."

She stared into his serious blue eyes, flabbergasted. How could he sit there so calmly while they discussed messing up Ellie's life for no good reason? They had no right playing God and telling Ellie she couldn't dance anymore. Did Josh even know that his sister's ballet career was over? He had to know, he was too intelligent not to. So how could he look so unfazed by taking away the only connection to dancing Ellie had left?

"She can find another gig," Josh added. "If she wants to dance in a nightclub, there are plenty of places in San Francisco that would hire her."

Vivian sighed. "What if she's not ready to go back?"

"Look," he said, rubbing her bare shoulder before pulling her closer to him. "We both know the car accident changed her life, but she can't hide away forever. She needs to rebuild her life."

Vivian grew quiet. Maybe he was right. If Ellie went home, she could finally begin putting the pieces of her life back together instead of pretending the accident never happened. And she'd have her big brother to lean on while she did that.

Seeing the situation in a new light, she said, "I think...you and Luke might be right. Hiding away in this town isn't the answer for Ellie."

"So you're going to do it? Fire her?"

She nodded. Tried to look past her own guilt and see the good that would come out of it. "I'll do it tomorrow."

"Thank you, Vivian."

"I'm not doing it for you, Josh."

"I know. But I'm still grateful." He brushed his hand over her face again, then slowly drew her into his arms and pressed his lips against hers. When he pulled back, he murmured, "Now maybe it's time we talk about what's happening between us."

Her palms grew damp. She knew it was a conversation they needed to have but it still made her apprehensive. They'd had one great date, sure. A few hot kisses, yes. And she couldn't forget how they'd nearly had sex in her living room the night before. But what did it all mean? She wasn't sure.

Josh had made it clear he wanted a relationship from her but could she really give that to him? She had no clue.

What she did know, however, was that she couldn't have this talk until she figured how she felt about it all.

"I need to go back to the club," she said, disentangling herself from his embrace. She stood up and reached for her purse, then swiped her cell phone from the coffee table. She glanced at Josh in time to see disappointment flashing across his face.

"You can't keep avoiding it, Viv."

"I'm not avoiding anything," she lied. "I really do need to go. I just came back for my cell. I'll probably be home late since we close at three, but we can talk tomorrow, okay?"

He rubbed the nape of his neck, looking frustrated, but after a moment his features relaxed. "Fine. We'll talk tomorrow."

Making it through dinner alive was the hardest thing Luke had ever done in his life. He hadn't been able to eat a bite, not when Ellie sat across from him in that traffic-stopping dress of hers. And concentration? Well, all that had flown right out the window once they left the restaurant and strolled toward the boardwalk, while his eyes stayed glued to her swaying hips and that enticing way her breasts bounced as she walked. When he'd realized she wasn't wearing a bra under that damn dress he'd almost made a run for it.

How on earth was he supposed to show her he was in control when he was far from it?

"I haven't been to a carnival in so long." There was a little spring to Ellie's stride as they approached the end of the boardwalk.

The carnival was set up on the outskirts of the little market Luke had yet to visit and as he and Ellie walked up to the entrance, she shot him a smile, looking elated by the noise and flashing lights. She'd been right; aside from a few children's rides, the enormous Ferris wheel seemed to be the only attraction, its lit-up cars sparkling under the dark sky.

But the game area made up for the lack of rides, offering everything from ring toss to target shooting to a We'll-guess-your-birthday stand. Luke had always enjoyed carnival games as a child, and immediately led Ellie in the direction of the loud mechanical rings and frustrated shouts.

"Look, the strength-o-meter," she said.

He followed her gaze and chuckled when he saw a heavy-set man cursing as he slammed a metal mallet against the platform. The meter shot up to Borderline Wimp, making high-pitched ringing sounds, as the man's date laughed in delight.

"I'd suggest you try it but we both know what a big, strong guy you are, don't we?" The suggestive tone of her voice caused a rush of warmth to pool in his groin.

So apparently the game was on. All throughout dinner he'd been wondering when Ellie would turn up the heat.

Hiding a smile, he took her hand and stroked it softly. Then enjoyed the way her eyes widened. "Why don't you pick the game then?"

Mischief danced across her face. "Okay, how about that one? Will you win me a goldfish?"

He followed her gaze to a nearby game stand, which required tossing a ring over a small fish bowl. "Not unless you plan on carrying that bowl around for the rest of the evening."

"Hmmm. You're right. Forget it. What should we do then?"

He gestured to the shooting range. "How about you win me a stuffed animal?"

"Shouldn't it be the other way around?"

He shot her a grin. "I just figured that a feminist like you would like to do the winning."

"A feminist?" She huffed. "All right, I'll show you how it's done."

They walked up to the counter, where Ellie paid the man and then reached for one of the shotguns. She looked at the owner warily. "These things aren't real, are they?"

"No, ma'am. They shoot BBs."

Awkwardly holding the gun, she turned her head. "The feminist confesses she's out of her element."

Well, well, it wasn't like Ellie to admit defeat. He took a step toward her. "Here, I'll show you how to hold it."

Unfortunately, in his line of work, carrying a firearm came with the job, and he'd taken dozens of weaponry courses over the years. He didn't like it, though. He'd never been comfortable with the power holding a gun wielded.

He approached Ellie from behind, and put his arms around her, clasping his fingers over hers. As his chest grazed her back, he heard her breath hitch, and the soft sound nearly caused him to keel over. It pleased him to no bounds how he got that reaction from her.

"Okay," he murmured. "Put your hands here." He moved her small hands over the gun. "Lower your head so that you can look through the scope. That's how you aim."

She lowered her head, the movement causing a stray strand of her hair to tickle his chin. "It's heavier than I thought." She twisted her head to shoot him a look hot enough to melt a glacier. "Harder, too."

"Is that a good or bad thing?" he returned roughly.

She ran her tongue over her bottom lip. "A good thing, of course. I like it hard."

Instant erection. Luckily his body was pressed against Ellie's back, shielding his enormous hard-on from carnival-goers. Then he had to rethink the word *lucky* as Ellie wiggled her ass against his crotch in obvious enjoyment to his predicament.

"What now?" she asked, turning to face the targets.

Now I take you to bed.

"How do I shoot?"

She's talking about the gun, you sex-crazed idiot.

"Now pick your target, check your aim, and gently squeeze the trigger."

"Do I have to be gentle?"

Luke thanked the lord above that she couldn't see the expression on his face. "Yes."

"Fine then." The gun made a quick popping sound as Ellie squeezed the trigger. She connected with one of the targets—a small milk bottle—and it toppled over with a crash.

"I hit it!"

The owner of the booth handed her a monstrous pink stuffed bunny and she held up her prize in triumph. Then she gave a slight frown. "I didn't think this through," she admitted with a glance at the enormous prize. "I'm not sure I want to carry this thing for the rest of the night."

He extended a hand. "I'll do it."

"No, I have a better idea." She took a few quick steps and intercepted a passing couple. With a smile, she bent in front of the little red-haired girl standing beside her parents and said, "Hey there, sweetie, how would you like to take this bunny off my hands?"

The girl, who couldn't have been older than five or six, looked up at her mother with big blue eyes. "Can I, Mama?"

The couple seemed less than thrilled at the prospect of carting that stuffed animal around but obviously neither one could say no to their daughter's angelic face. Ellie handed the bunny to the girl and the small family strolled off. With another smile, she turned to Luke. "Those parents probably hate me."

"They didn't look excited about the three-foot-tall bunny," he agreed.

Ellie just shrugged and let her gaze roam the lit-up

grounds. "Okay, what should we do next?"

"How about the Ferris wheel?"

She blanched. "I'll pass."

"Don't tell me you don't like Ferris wheels."

"No, Ferris wheels are fine. It's heights that bother me."

He couldn't keep the challenge out of his voice. "Ellie Dawson, scared of heights? Scared of anything, for that matter? Shocking."

"Everyone has their weakness."

He had to give her that. His weakness, ironically, was standing right in front of him.

"Come on," he coaxed. "Let's go for a ride."

Ha! Looked like she wasn't the only one who'd mastered the art of double entendres. He silently applauded himself for the situation he'd just placed her in. If she said no, it would be as if she was saying no to the *other* ride, the one that had the two of them naked, in bed, burning up the sheets.

He almost rubbed his hands together in glee, knowing from the nervous expression on her face that she was about to back down.

Or maybe not.

"Okay. One ride." She licked her lips again then lifted her hand to his face and ran it along the curve of his jaw. "You'll protect me, won't you, Luke?"

His entire mouth went dry but he still managed to give her the cool, confident look he'd perfected over the years.

"Of course I'll protect you."

Chapter Nine

"Why aren't we moving?"

Ellie clung to Luke's arm in terror as their Ferris wheel car hovered fifteen feet off the ground, swaying dangerously from side to side. Though they weren't too high up yet, her nerves skittered like a timid hare in the presence of a mountain lion. Just seeing the tops of people's heads made her uneasy, confirming her belief that human beings had legs and feet for a reason, and that's so they could stand on solid land.

"They're still letting people on. The ride hasn't started yet."

Luke's patient tone didn't soothe her. She glanced up at the inky-black sky, trying to focus on the white stars sparkling overhead. Looking up, however, only strengthened the realization that she was up too. Not down, on land, where she belonged.

"Let's get off," she burst out, her head growing light as the car swayed in the breeze.

Really smooth, Ellie. Way to keep up the sexy vixen act. It just figured, didn't it? She'd been doing so well, throwing out provocative little remarks, eliciting a hard-on from Luke, and he'd had to turn the tables by bringing her on this damn Ferris wheel.

Luke shot her a sideways look, not bothering to hide his half-smile. "Relax, Elenore. Nothing's going to happen. You're safe."

She wrung her hands together, cursing herself for her fear. Heights had always bothered her, though she didn't have an insightful story that revealed why. No past experience, no little anecdotes, no deep-rooted trauma. All she knew was each time she was more than two feet off the ground, her body went numb with panic.

She heard a gate slam, and before she could blink, the car soared upwards. Her stomach churned as they continued to rise, dangling hundreds of feet off the ground.

"I might be sick."

Luke laughed. "You won't be sick."

She grabbed his arm and dug her fingernails in his bare skin and the feathery dark hair over it. "Don't laugh."

"Why not?"

"When you laugh, the car shakes. And when the car shakes, my stomach hurts and my—"

"Ellie, calm down."

The car stopped. It did that every few seconds so the passengers could enjoy the view. Ellie, on the other hand, was enjoying nothing. Not even the sight of the ocean, midnight blue under the dark sky, or the quaint little houses and huts in the distance, could ease her nerves. Sucking in a breath, she squeezed Luke's arm tighter, riddled with anxiety.

"Okay, you need to distract me, Luke. Seriously."

He sighed. "How?"

"I don't know. Talk. Tell me something."

"What do you want to know?"

For a split second, she forgot all about their location after his easy-going answer. She couldn't remember the last time he'd been so willing to talk about himself, and no matter how terrified she was at the moment, she couldn't pass up the chance to get into his head.

Or his heart.

"Are you seeing anyone back in San Francisco?" The question slipped out before she could stop it.

"I was." He raked his fingers through his dark hair. "But not anymore."

"What happened?"

Discomfort flickered in his gray eyes, followed by a flash of bitterness. "I broke things off."

"Why?" When he didn't answer, she met his gaze. "Please tell me. Otherwise I'll start panicking again."

"Let's just say Robin wasn't who I thought she was." He shifted in his seat, and his shoulder brushed against hers. A rush of heat sizzled through her skin, spreading downward until the juncture between her thighs ached. God, would she ever get used to being this close to Luke?

"Who was she then?"

"A wonderful liar, for one."

She didn't answer. Just waited for him to continue. Hoped that he would.

"She wanted to marry me."

"Did you want to marry her?"

His eyes darkened. "Not at first. Not until she told me she was pregnant."

She bit back a gasp. Pregnant? Luke had gotten a woman pregnant and broken off the relationship?

"She wasn't, by the way. Pregnant." He shot her a knowing

glance. "That was her big lie."

"God, Luke, that's awful."

She tried to hold back the fury rising in her throat. The rage. His revelation made her spine stiffen. That a woman would lie about being pregnant just to trap a man into marriage sickened her. It was a slap in the face, another reminder that she'd never be able to provide a man with children. While women like Luke's ex flaunted their fertility and used it for their own selfish gain. If there was one thing she'd learned these last painful six months, it was that children were a gift. Not a bartering chip.

She felt pressure on her arm. Luke's hand, big and warm. The look of concern on his face told her that her anger was written all over hers.

"You okay?"

She let out a breath. "I'm fine. I'm just...disgusted by what your ex-girlfriend did."

The car ascended again, until they were at the very top of the wheel. The height was death defying, yet a nagging pang of curiosity distracted her from looking down. She wanted to voice her thoughts and ask Luke the question biting at her lips, but was fearful of the answer. Desperate for it at the same time.

"Luke..." She bit her lower lip. "Were you disappointed?"

His gray eyes looked almost black under the night sky. "About what?"

"Not being a father." The question choked out of her throat.

He didn't answer for a long time, just turned his head and looked in the distance. She admired his strong profile as her fingers tingled with the urge to touch him. Five o'clock shadow dotted his jaw, making him appear rugged and very, very masculine. For the first time all evening, she smelled his aftershave, the spicy scent tickling her nose, adding to the attraction building inside her.

He was so different from any of her high school boyfriends. From Scott and his boyish good looks and childish attitude. Luke was all man. Six feet and one hundred and seventy pounds of pure, unadulterated *male*.

She shivered. They were sitting so close right now that all she had to do was turn her head, lean forward an inch and she would feel his lips on hers. Yet her question hung in the air, overpowering her desire, and her chest felt tight, as if her entire life depended on his answer.

"Yeah," he finally said, meeting her eyes again. "I guess I was a little disappointed."

A long breath seeped from her lungs, tinged with regret. Well, of course he would want children. As strong and powerful as he was, he was also tender. Gentle. Luke would be a good father, she'd never deny that. But she couldn't control the pain she felt at his reply. Knowing she would never be the woman who gave him a child. Wondering why that was even important.

She suddenly had the urge to confide in him about her own situation, but the reality of her future sunk in and she knew sharing her sorrow with him wasn't an option. What would be the point? To see the pity in his eyes when she told him she was barren? The sympathy when she revealed her days of ballet were over? No, thank you. She didn't want or need anyone's goddamn sympathy or pity. Not even Luke's.

"It would be nice, I guess," he continued, oblivious to her turmoil. "A few of the people I've protected had kids, and I always enjoyed being around them." He shrugged. "But my own? Sure, I'd like it, just not now. And certainly not with a woman who'd lie and scheme to get me to settle down."

A silence fell as the car started its descent. Ellie couldn't understand what she was feeling or why her chest ached this way. She didn't speak as the attendant pulled open the safety bar, or when Luke held her arm and helped her off the platform. They walked past the line of people waiting to get onto the ride, silent, until Luke finally spoke.

"It's getting late. Let me take you home."

Standing under the glowing yellow porch light of Ellie's bungalow, Luke realized he didn't want the night to end. He watched as she rummaged around in her purse for her keys, wondering if she'd invite him in. Three hours ago he would've been surprised *not* to receive an invitation, but the moment they finished their stint on the Ferris wheel, Ellie had done a complete one-eighty.

No more flirting. No more sexy grins. No more sinful innuendos. She'd simply clammed up, became distant and made no further mention of the ultimatum she'd given him earlier.

Had she changed her mind about sleeping with him? Funny, how his plan had been all about getting her to back down, but now that she had, he was strangely disappointed.

"Jeez, it's amazing how difficult it is to find anything in this purse," she mumbled, rolling her eyes as she pulled out her key chain. "And all I've got in here is a wallet and some gum."

She stuck the key in the lock, turned it, and opened the door. He held his breath, wondering what would happen next. Would it be *Goodnight, Luke* or *Come in?*

Goodnight. It had to be that. He had no business wanting to prolong the evening. He'd already won. She'd backed down. Now was the time to return to the motel and devise another way to convince her to come home.

"So..." Her soft voice trailed off as she glanced up at him.

The porch light framed her face like a halo, making her blue eyes shine and her dark hair lighten to a deep caramel. "Viv cancelled the second show and I don't plan on going to sleep yet. Would you like to come in for a cup of coffee?"

Say no.

"Sure."

Idiot.

He sighed and followed her into the darkened front hall, grateful that at least there hadn't been any sexual undertones to her offer. She really did seem to have changed her mind. As they headed inside he found himself engaging in his new favorite past time—watching her ass sway as she walked. His mouth watered at each stolen glimpse.

She flicked on the light, and a warm glow filled the living room. He looked around and absorbed the cozy atmosphere Ellie had created. All the cluttered bookshelves reminded him of how much she liked to read, and as he stepped toward her CD rack, his eyes roamed over the numerous classical titles.

Did she put on one of these CDs at night? Mozart, maybe? Did she slip into her old leotards and dance by herself?

"How do you take your coffee?" She slipped out of her sandals, kicked them aside, and then edged barefoot toward the doorway of the kitchen.

"Black."

Her mouth tilted in a knowing smile. "Of course. I'll be right back."

He made himself comfortable on the plush sofa, listening to the sounds of Ellie bustling around the kitchen. She was only gone for a few moments, yet her absence bothered him. It wasn't until she reentered the room with two steaming mugs in her hands that he relaxed again.

She handed him one of the mugs, then settled on the opposite edge of the couch. "Careful, it's hot."

He watched as she blew over the rim of her cup, the cool puffs of air from her mouth blending with the steam rising from the hot liquid. Then, curling her knees beneath her, she took a hesitant sip before placing the cup on the coffee table.

"What did you mean when you said 'of course'?" he asked. "Is there something wrong with the way I drink my coffee?"

She shrugged, causing her long dark strands to cascade over her shoulders. Her hair looked silky to the touch. Luke's fingers tingled.

"It just wasn't surprising you drink it black," she replied. "You know, how a person drinks their coffee tells a lot about them."

He looked at her with interest. "Really?"

"Sure. Take Josh, for instance. He claims he likes it black, being the big strong tough guy he is." She grinned. "But when no one's looking, he dumps in a few sugar cubes. Tough guy hiding his soft side."

"What does my preference say about me?"

The tip of her tongue darted out and licked the seams of her lips. "Well, black implies strength, maybe some bitterness."

"I'm not bitter," he interjected.

She ignored him. "It hints at stubbornness too. But look at the way you drink it. You hold the cup tightly, again implying strength, but your sips are slow, methodical almost. You like to be in control, even in the way you drink your coffee. But you swallow slowly, as if savoring the liquid, however bitter it is."

"And what does that say?" he asked, strangely fascinated.

"I don't know. Respect? Appreciation?"

He set down his mug and folded his hands over his lap. It

was a little unnerving how she'd just pegged him completely on the basis of how he drank his coffee. Stubborn, he was that all right. Controlled? Hell, yeah. Though he'd never realized coffee could convey all that.

"What about you?" he said suddenly. "What does your drink say about you?"

"Nothing."

"What do you mean, nothing?"

She gave an impish smile that lit up her whole face. "I don't drink coffee." She held out her cup. "See, tea."

He rolled his eyes. "On the contrary, I bet tea says a lot about you."

"Fine. Tell me."

There she was again, the sassy Ellie he'd always liked. Her blue eyes glimmered with challenge and amusement and before he could stop himself he moved closer to her. His thigh grazed hers. Too close yet not close enough.

"Well, you're gentle, soft." He dipped his head and breathed in the aroma of her tea. "Sweet, too."

She snorted, and the sound brought a smile to his lips. "Gentle, soft and sweet? I can't say I've ever been described as that before."

He held up his hand. "I wasn't finished. Give me the cup." She handed it over and he took a long sip. "See, no sugar. It's flavored, but a little bitter. Strength." He took another sip. "With a hint of cinnamon. Spicy." He finally gave her back the cup.

"You're pretty good at this." She laughed. "Maybe we should go into business together, ripping off strangers with fake drink fortunes."

She placed the cup on the table again and looked at him, her mouth open as if she was about to say something. Before she could, he cut her off, the words slipping out of his mouth before he could stop them.

"Dance for me."

Her eyes widened. "What?"

"I want to see you dance." He swallowed against the dryness of his throat. "Do you have any of your old ballet costumes here?"

Shadows and clouds danced across her face. "Yes."

"Put one on. Put on one of your CDs. I want to see you dance ballet again, Ellie."

He didn't know where any of it came from, just that he needed to watch her dance. What she did at the club was appealing to the eye—among other things—but it wasn't Ellie. She was elegant, graceful as a swan, agile as a gymnast. It had come out of left field, but he suddenly knew he couldn't leave without watching her be a ballerina again.

"I can't."

She rose from the sofa and walked across the room, pausing in front of one of the bookshelves. Aimlessly running her fingers over the spines of the hard covers, she let out a shaky breath, her back to him.

He stood up and approached her. "Why not? Don't you want to dance again? You love ballet, you always have."

Her lips tightened in a firm line, her jaw tense. "I still do, Luke."

"Then dance for me."

"I can't."

He took a step toward the CD rack and pulled out the first case he saw. "Come on, Elenore. Here, *Swan Lake*. Just one song." He held out the CD.

She stared at the disk as if it were a bomb. Breathing

deeply, her chest contracting, her blue eyes darkening to cobalt. Then, to his shock, she grabbed the CD and threw it across the room. The case shattered against the wall, breaking apart then falling to the hardwood floor. A dull silence descended over the room, save for Ellie's ragged breathing.

Her eyes were wild, angry, and all he could do was stare at her in utter disbelief.

"Get out, Luke."

The sharpness of her voice shocked him. "I'm sorry I asked you to dance. I didn't think it would be a—"

"I can't!" She nearly roared at him, her brown hair flying in all directions as she stalked past him. She began to pace, quickly, desperately, while her dress swirled like a tornado over her thighs. "Don't you get it? I *physically can't.*"

He'd never seen her look this volatile. He watched as she stopped pacing and stood there shaking in front of him. Her hands balled into fists, her mouth twisted in a bitter smile. And all he could say was, "What?"

"My foot, Luke." She looked at him as if he was a complete imbecile. "Remember the foot I broke in the accident?"

"But it healed."

"Healed, yeah." She gave a harsh laugh. "But it'll never be strong enough again. You know that thing we ballerinas do, standing on our tiptoes and fluttering around? That's called *en pointe.* And I can't do it anymore. I can't dance ballet. So if you think I'm going to put on a tutu and lunge across the room in graceful pirouettes, you're a fool."

She finished with a long, trembling breath. Slowly, she uncurled her fists, her fingers falling limply, hands dangling beside her hips. Shock filled his entire body as her revelation swarmed his brain like an army of bees. She couldn't dance? Like the pieces of a puzzle fitting together, he understood.

143

That's why she'd left the ballet company. Not because she didn't want to be there. But because she couldn't.

The pain in her eyes cut him to the core. The spark in there had burned out, leaving deep blue pools laced with sorrow and...shame? Staring into her pain-filled face, his heart squeezed and ached. He knew how important dancing was to her. Since she was a kid, all she'd talked about was how she would be a prima ballerina someday. He imagined her devastation at learning that could never happen, and suddenly felt like a complete jerk for what he'd done.

Dance for me.

I can't.

"Ellie, I'm sorry."

When she didn't answer, he walked toward her, eliminating the distance between them. Her cheeks were red, flushed from her outburst, and he could feel the heat emanating from her body. Stepping even closer, he cupped her face with his hands, ignoring the way her eyes widened again.

"Is that why you left San Francisco?"

She swallowed. "Yes."

"You should've told me. You should've told Josh."

She shrugged his hands from her face. "What would that have achieved?"

"We could have helped you."

"How?" Sarcasm dripped from her voice. "Can you fix my foot? Make it all better? Amazing, because I went to three physical therapists who couldn't do a damn thing for me."

His nostrils flared. He didn't like the way she was talking to him. Cold, sarcastic, as if she'd given up, as if not being able to dance implied her life was over.

"So please, don't patronize me." She huffed out a breath.

"In fact, just go. I want you to leave."

He set his jaw. "No."

"Yes. You know why I'm here, so now there's no reason for you to stick around."

A part of him knew she was absolutely right. He'd finally figured out what was wrong, why she'd taken off and left her old life behind her. He could leave, tell Josh the truth, and be on his way. But another part refused to go. Rooted to his feet, he stared into her blue eyes that still glimmered with anger, bitterness and regret. How could he leave when all he wanted to do was take her into his arms?

"Go, Luke."

"No," he said again.

And then he pulled her toward him and captured her mouth with his. He pried her lips open with his tongue and plunged inside. In the back of his mind, a voice told him to slow down. Not to push her. Be gentle.

His mind swam in a sea of desire, and it wasn't until her soft hands wrapped around his neck that he realized she was kissing him back. Fervently. Desperately. Their tongues dueled, greedily taking and demanding.

Still devouring her mouth, he slid his other hand down her small, warm body, crumpled the hem of her dress with his fist and shoved it up to her waist.

She wasn't wearing panties.

He managed a strangled "Jesus Christ" as heat rushed through his blood. Then he rubbed his palm over her slick folds.

The air grew heavy with tension and sexual promise. Stifling a groan, he dropped to his knees and started kissing her smooth thighs. He dragged his tongue over her clit, enjoying the soft moans that exited her mouth. He wanted to bring her over the edge, make her come with his tongue, but his erection was too hard to ignore. After a few more licks, he rose to his feet and kissed her again.

Moaning again, Ellie unzipped his jeans, shoved them down and stroked his cock. A guttural groan choked out of his throat.

"I want you inside," she murmured.

She didn't have to ask him twice. He grabbed his jeans off the floor and pulled out the condom he'd stashed in the back pocket. He tried guiding her toward the hallway leading to the bedroom, but she shoved her tongue in his mouth again, making it difficult to breathe, let alone walk. Finally he stumbled forward and pushed her against the wall, and then he was back between her thighs, entering her with a quick thrust that had them both gasping.

"Oh fuck," he groaned.

It was all going too fast, and yet too damn slow. Unable to control himself, he gripped her firm ass and pounded into her, fucking her hard. He held back, miraculously, until Ellie shuddered with release, and then he joined her over the edge. His orgasm ripped through him, searing every nerve ending and making him dizzy with pleasure.

Breathing heavily, he slowly pulled out, then chuckled when Ellie gave a small disappointed whimper.

A moment later the chuckle died in his throat. As his eyes regained focus, the sight of Ellie smashed into his chest like a sledgehammer. Her back against the wall, her dress hiked up, one breast exposed. Goddamn it, was he a Neanderthal? He'd just taken her standing up and screwed the hell out of her as if she was nothing more than a toy for his own pleasure.

Jerking back, he hissed out a breath. She'd told him her career was over, and instead of comforting her, he'd jumped her without once thinking about her feelings.

"God, Ellie, I'm sorry."

He awkwardly rolled the condom off his dick and knelt down to pick up his jeans. He hadn't even taken the time to remove his boxers, for fuck's sake. What was the matter with him?

Shame coursed through his veins as he pulled his jeans up and zipped them. He wanted to say something more, apologize once more, but he lost his capacity for speech again as he watched Ellie gently push her breast back into the bodice of her dress and smooth the skirt down over her legs.

The questioning look in her blue eyes caused something inside of him to squeeze. Damn, she was beautiful. Achingly beautiful.

"Ellie." His voice was hoarse and tinged with regret. "I'm sorry," he said again, swallowing. "I should go."

Chapter Ten

Twenty-four hours after Luke ravished her body, Ellie wondered if she'd simply imagined the whole thing. Maybe she'd fantasized it, or maybe she'd accidentally dropped a couple of tabs of LSD in her tea last night and hallucinated everything that followed.

It happened. Deal with it.

Ellie sighed and rolled her stocking up to her thigh. God, it would be so much easier believing it didn't happen. At least then she wouldn't have to wonder why he'd deserted her like that.

"You coming?" Marlene's voice startled her. With a tilt of her head, she saw Marlene lingering near the dressing room door.

"I'll be out in a sec," Ellie answered. "Go on out."

Marlene's heels clicked against the floor as she left the room, and once the sound faded Ellie sank into her chair and welcomed the silence. She studied her reflection in the mirror then lifted her hand to her lips. Swollen. Still swollen from Luke's mouth crushing them.

God, would she ever be able to understand that infuriating man? Every time she came into contact with Luke, whether they were bickering or kissing, her body felt like a Mack truck had hit it. No other man got to her like that. Irritated the hell out of her and made her crazy with lust at the same time.

How could he just walk out on her last night? Since he'd come to town, it had become almost a habit—kissing her, touching her, and then hurrying off like a dog with his tail between his legs. But scampering away after giving her the best sex of her life? That was unacceptable. Not to mention insensitive.

What was the matter with that man? She'd just revealed her ballet career was over, she'd given her body to him, and he'd left. He'd *left*.

A part of her still couldn't believe she'd told him the truth. Well, some of the truth, anyway, since she'd refrained from mentioning the hysterectomy. But telling him about that...well, it wasn't an option.

Every time she thought about their conversation up on that Ferris wheel her chest tightened with disappointment. But damn it, why did she feel that way? She and Luke weren't a couple. They never would be. He didn't want to settle down, especially with his best friend's sister.

And besides, how could she get involved with someone when she didn't even know who the hell she was anymore? The accident had taken so much from her. Her career. Her fiancé. Her ability to have children. Who exactly was she, without all those things?

Definitely not the same person she'd been before she lost them, that's for sure.

"You shouldn't have come in tonight."

The sound of Vivian's brisk voice broke through her troubling thoughts, quickly bringing on a new set of troubled thoughts. Ellie still hadn't questioned Viv about the dark-haired younger man Marlene's cousin had spotted her with, but she couldn't shake the feeling that it had been Luke. She hadn't bought Luke's explanation about his conversation with Viv last night—the two of them looked too serious to be discussing a carnival—but Ellie hadn't wanted to push him then. She'd been too focused on turning up the heat and turning Luke on.

Well, she'd turned him on, all right.

And he'd rushed off like a coward.

"Why shouldn't I have come in?" Ellie asked with a glance to Viv's reflection in the vanity mirror.

As usual, her boss looked absolutely gorgeous in her work attire—a pale-blue silk shirt, tan slacks, and three-inch heels. But the look on her face wasn't the usual one of excitement and encouragement she normally wore before a show. Right now she just came across as weary.

"I've been doing a lot of thinking since our talk yesterday," Vivian replied.

"What about it?"

"I think giving you this job at the club might have been a mistake."

A wave of panic crept up her throat as she saw the serious look in her boss's eyes. Was she firing her? Her panic doubled at the thought. She couldn't lose this job. It was all she had left, the only thing that made living in San Valdez worthwhile. And Vivian. She couldn't lose her either. These past two months, Viv had been her saving grace, the one person she could count on.

"What are you saying?"

"Yesterday I realized you're here to escape. To hide. And, honey, I think you're hiding away for the wrong reasons."

"I'm not hiding away."

"Yes, you are. Your jerk of an ex fed you a line of bull about your life being over, and you bought it. I'm beginning to think..." Vivian took a breath. "That your brother and Luke are right, that you should be at home."

Alarm spilled over her. No, not Vivian too. She should've never told her boss the real story behind the car accident.

"Ellie, I can't stand by and watch you waste your life away."

"How am I wasting my life away?" she protested. "And what does that say about you? You live here too."

Vivian smiled softly. "Honey, I may be forty-four, but I had some life. I raised an amazing kid, worked my ass off and took a few trips to Vegas that one day I'll tell you about. I chose to retire here, to run this club and enjoy the relaxation this small town has to offer. But you, you're still young. You have the rest of your life ahead of you. Don't waste it away here."

"I like it here." She swallowed back a lump of pain, knowing deep down that there was some truth in her words. She did love San Valdez, but a part of her missed her life in San Francisco. Her condo. Her friends. Even her annoying brother.

But she wasn't going to tell Vivian that. She wasn't ready to go back yet, if she ever would be, and right now leaving this little beach town and going home to face the world terrified her.

Vivian reached down and ruffled her hair. "I know you do, but I won't be the one to hold you back. There's so much you can do with your life. Not being able to dance ballet doesn't mean your career is over. You can become an instructor, open your own ballet school. And you should think about getting involved with a man again."

"I will. One day I'll do all that." She steadied her voice in an attempt to keep the desperation out of it.

"And when is *one day*? A year from now? Two?"

"I don't know." Her throat suddenly felt tight and in the mirror she saw the sheen of unshed tears in her eyes.

"I'm sorry, honey, but I think you should go back to San Francisco."

A single tear spilled out and slid down her cheek. "Are you firing me?"

The obvious look of regret on Viv's face didn't make her answer any less hurtful. "Yes. I won't let you hide out here, so I guess that means I'm letting you go."

As the full significance of her boss's words settled in, Ellie clamped her mouth closed to keep a sob from slipping out. How could Vivian look so calm? How could she fire her without even blinking?

She sat there, waiting for Vivian to smile and say "gotcha" but it didn't happen. It was only when Vivian uttered a soft, "I'm sorry" and headed for the door that a startling question hit her.

"Just answer one thing," Ellie burst out. She twisted in her chair and watched as her ex-boss turned to face her. "Was this Luke's idea?"

"No." Vivian didn't even hesitate.

Despite the relief filling her stomach she still wasn't soothed. "Then why were you having dinner with him yesterday evening?"

"What?" Vivian furrowed her brows in confusion. "I didn't have dinner with Luke. I was—" Her sentence came to an abrupt halt, bringing another wave of suspicion to Ellie's gut.

"You were what, Viv? Marlene's cousin saw you with a dark-haired guy. Who was he?"

Vivian opened her mouth then snapped it shut.

In a tone dripping with bitterness, Ellie managed a low taunt. "Come on, who were you with?"

It seemed like an eternity before she finally got her answer. "I was with Josh."

Her spine stiffened. "Josh?" she echoed. "As in my brother, Josh?"

"Yes."

Not even the guilty look on Viv's face and the apologetic tone of her voice could stop the rush of red-hot betrayal that sliced through Ellie's chest. Vivian and Josh? Her best friend, the one person she'd leaned on all these months, was in cahoots with her brother?

"How long has he been in town?" she asked through clenched teeth.

"A few days."

"I see."

Vivian stepped closer, her green eyes swimming with regret. "He just came here to make sure you were—"

Ellie held up her hand and shot the other woman a silencing—and icy—stare. "I don't need your explanations." She locked her jaw in an attempt to stop its trembling. "If you'll excuse me, I need to get ready for the show. It's my final curtain call, after all."

"Ellie—"

"I. Need. To. Get. Ready." Each word emerged as a ragged gasp.

"All right. We'll...talk later then?"

The fury clogging her throat prevented an answer from coming out so she simply fixed a cold expression on her face and waited. Waited for Viv to leave the room. Waited for it all to sink in. Waited until she was alone before finally allowing the tears to fall.

"Don't go in there."

Luke stopped in his tracks at the sight of Vivian's red-rimmed eyes and pale face. He'd been on his way to Ellie's dressing room after finally working up the nerve to see her. He knew he and Ellie needed to talk about what happened between them last night and he didn't appreciate Vivian intercepting him. No matter how distraught she looked.

"I really need to speak to her," he answered, reaching for the doorknob.

Vivian stopped his hand. Her grip felt cold. "Now is really not the time, Luke. She's upset."

"Why is—" He stopped suddenly as the answer dawned on him. "You fired her, didn't you?"

The older blonde's small nod and dejected expression caused a wave of cold regret to swell in his chest. Damn. When he'd asked Vivian to fire Ellie yesterday he hadn't known what would happen at the bungalow. His despicable behavior had no doubt hurt her, but add to that the loss of her job and...well, he now understood why Vivian seemed so devastated. Though her devastation probably didn't even compare to Ellie's.

"Did you tell her I asked you to do it?"

"No. She was angry enough as it was. Especially when I told her Josh was in town."

Luke resisted from slapping his forehead with his hand. This was just wonderful. "I should go in there." He rested his hand on the door handle and this time didn't get any resistance from Vivian. She moved past him. Her high heels made soft clicking noises as she walked toward the end of the hall and disappeared through the doorway leading into the main room.

Luke closed his eyes briefly, suddenly regretting he'd ever asked Vivian to take away Ellie's job. The fluorescent lights overhead hissed and crackled, making his head hurt. A part of him wanted to turn around and leave the club, leave this goddamn town and forget he'd ever come here, but he knew he couldn't do that. He owed it to Ellie to stick around a bit longer. He also owed her a whopper of an apology.

Not only that, but it was time to end this insanity. He'd fulfilled his end of the deal and he planned on collecting.

Opening his eyes, he released a long breath and entered the dressing room.

"Ellie."

The sound of Luke's whiskey-rough voice from the doorway startled her. With a quick gulp, she wiped her eyes with the handkerchief on the vanity table and blinked back her tears. Oh God, she didn't need this. Not now. Not when she felt so vulnerable and exposed.

"I, uh, just ran into Vivian in the hallway," he added, crossing the room with measured strides until he stood only a few feet away.

"I suppose she told you she fired me."

"Yeah, she told me."

"Did she tell you my brother is in town?" She narrowed her eyes. "Or did you already know that?"

"I found out yesterday. Apparently he's been laying low at Vivian's house."

"I can't believe she lied to me. I thought she cared about me, that—" Ellie stopped as a wave of sickness crept up her stomach and burned its way up to her throat. She didn't want to think about any of this right now. Despite the fact that she was out of a job, she still had one more show to put on, and the acid searing her chest and the pain pulsing through her head wouldn't help her do that.

She rose from the chair and kept her expression cool and

detached. Luke didn't move closer but she saw his gaze sweep over her corset and skirt. It irked her that his eyes didn't have that spark of lust in them, the way they'd gleamed the first night he saw her in this costume. Now he just looked remorseful.

God, she didn't want to have this conversation with him, didn't want to hear his half-assed apologies. Last night he'd fled, left her half-naked, aroused and confused, and it would take a lot more than *I'm sorry* to make her forget that.

"What are you doing here?" she finally said with a sigh. She picked an imaginary spot of lint off her skirt, refusing to meet his eyes.

"First, apologizing."

No kidding. "And what could you possibly be apologizing for?" she returned with a scowl.

"I'm sorry about last night."

"No, really? This seems to be a running theme with you, Lucas. Kissing me, running off. Screwing me, running off. And then, of course, the sincere apology the next day."

He ignored her sarcastic tone. "I was out of line yesterday."

She let out a frustrated breath. "Why do you say that?"

A look of confusion crossed his handsome features. "Because of the way I acted." He coughed. "Treating you like that. Mauling you like some kind of animal."

She just stared at him. He really was an idiot. Had he been completely oblivious to her arousal? She'd been wet for him, she'd come apart in his arms, she'd had a body-numbing orgasm. He was a fool if he thought the desire, the raw need, had been one-sided.

"Did you hear me complaining?" she burst out, surprised by the harshness of her voice.

"I just thought..."

Her frustration only increased at the bewilderment flickering in his eyes. Planting her hands on her hips, she marched toward him. "You thought that you were taking advantage of me? Having your way with Josh's poor little sister?" She gave a groan that bordered on a growl. "For God's sake, Luke!"

"I practically tore your clothes off."

The regret in his eyes turned her frustration into fury. "Did you ever stop to think that maybe I *liked* it? That maybe, just maybe, I wanted you too? Damn it, Luke, I've wanted you for fifteen years. Fifteen years!"

"I thought—"

"And have you forgotten about that orgasm you gave me last night? Since we're being so honest here, I want you to know I've never come that hard in my life."

Her admission hung in the air, mingling with the long gust of air she exhaled from her lungs. Sparks flew from her eyes as her heart thudded against her ribs. God, it felt good to say that.

As shock filled his face, power surged through her. She'd gotten to him. Caught him off-guard. Caused some of his irritating self-control to chip. And it felt great.

"Now what's second?" she asked, crossing her arms in a tight vice over her chest.

He coughed again. "What do you mean?"

"You said the apology was first. So what the hell is second?"

He shifted, looking uncomfortable. "Well, we did have a deal, remember?"

She arched both eyebrows.

"At your house, you said I give you one night and you'd

come home. Well, I did my part and now it's your turn to—"

"Excuse me?" she interrupted. "You most certainly didn't do your part. I asked for one *night.* I got a five-minute fuck and then you rushed off without even saying goodbye."

"Damn it, Ellie. Like you said, you got what you wanted, right?"

Pure ice pumped through her bloodstream. "Seeing your back as you stumbled out the door was not what I wanted. Which means the deal's off, Luke. Not only is it off, but it won't be on the table again, I can guarantee that."

She wasn't sure if his face was red with frustration or anger, but she didn't care. Lifting her chin, she shuffled past him, all the while feeling his gaze burning into her back.

"I need to get on stage," she announced without turning around. She didn't dare to look at him, didn't want to see his expression or hear his arguments.

For the first time in weeks, she'd shown Luke Russell exactly who was boss.

I've wanted you for fifteen years.

The words ran through Luke's head as he strode toward a table near the stage and sank down. Damn, he needed to sit, his body still winded from Ellie's confession. He wasn't a stranger to surprises—life as a bodyguard was full of them—but he couldn't remember ever being this stunned.

Fifteen years? She'd wanted him for that long? He'd always suspected she had a crush on him when she was a kid, but once she hit her teens, he figured she'd gotten over it. When she'd fallen in love with Whelan, it had been as much as confirmed. And now she decided to tell him she'd wanted him all along?

Like you didn't know.

After days of ignoring the nagging little voice in his head, he finally listened to it. He knew he affected her, had known it since the night he'd kissed her out in the alley, when her warm needy response had been evident. Last night, too, she'd responded. He remembered cupping her dampness, hearing her breathy moans, the feel of her hand on his erection, the way her wet heat had clamped against him. Her cries of pleasure as she came.

He'd run out of there thinking he'd hurt her, used her, but the memory of her encouraging gaze and soft pleas told a different story.

She'd wanted him as much as he'd wanted her.

Luke fought back a wave of desperation as the lights dimmed and the curtains lifted. Damn it. He didn't like being left hanging. Didn't like having to sit here and think about Ellie's bombshell. Analyze what it meant and why it made him feel so...happy.

And he certainly didn't like the way she'd made their agreement null and void based on a stupid technicality. So he hadn't stayed the night. She'd still gotten what she'd wanted. Still taken a sledgehammer to all the control he'd built over the years and utterly demolished it. He wondered how he'd ever explain this to Josh. *I had sex with your little sister but she still won't come home.*

Fortunately he was pretty sure Josh didn't own a gun.

Shaking his head, he forced everything out of his mind and focused his gaze on the stage. The dancers were doing a routine that reminded him of *A Chorus Line*. High kicks, sexy spins and a lot of ass wiggling.

"Look at the ass on that one."

The man at the neighboring table turned to Luke with a

massive leer on his pudgy face. Luke's nostrils flared as he followed the man's extended finger and saw one of the dancers shake her mesh-covered bottom. "You know," he couldn't help but snap, "she has a name. A face too."

The man cocked his head and grinned in Luke's direction. "With a body like that, who gives a damn about her face?"

He breathed deeply, willing his anger to dissolve. A barrage of comebacks bit at his tongue but he finally decided the balding, middle-aged creep wasn't worth it. He turned away, ignoring the man next to him and trying to ignore how sexy Ellie looked up on that stage. When a flash of movement from the doorway caught his attention, he shifted his gaze completely.

Was that...? Why yes it was. The Latin heartthrob Ellie had gone out with a couple days ago walked through the door, followed by a shorter, light-skinned man. Luke's eyebrows shot up to his forehead as the two men walked, hand-in-hand, toward a booth across the room and sat down. Disbelief creased his features.

The little witch.

He choked back a laugh as the memory of Ellie dancing with her date flashed across his brain. Had he been too consumed with jealousy to pick up on the guy's more than obvious sexual orientation, or was he just an idiot? Or maybe Ellie Dawson simply knew him too well.

He shook his head, unable to fight the grin that swept over his face. He had to hand it to her, she was good. She'd played him like a fiddle. That date had been nothing but a farce and he'd fallen for it.

And yet instead of being angry with her, he was left feeling impressed by her sneakiness and desperately relieved that the other man had never been a threat to him.

It was the latter emotion that troubled the hell out of him.

As the other dancers bustled into the dressing room Ellie hung back. She rubbed her forehead, suddenly feeling light-headed. Not to mention absolutely hollow inside. When she'd walked off the stage she'd seen Vivian standing at the bar and for a moment their gazes had locked. Her friend's silent plea had tugged at Ellie's heart, made her want to rush over to Viv and give her a hug. But she hadn't been able to do it, not when she still couldn't stop those feelings of betrayal from pulsing through her.

Not only had Vivian fired her but she'd lied about Josh being in town, and that wasn't something Ellie could get over so easily. Or quickly.

Hugging her chest with her arms, she walked toward the back doors and stepped into the alley, needing to breathe in the cool night air. She had to collect her thoughts, figure out what she was going to do now that she didn't have a job. Now that everything was up in the air with Luke.

God, what am I doing here?

Out of nowhere, a wave of homesickness so powerful, so torrential, crashed over her body. The light evening breeze snaked through her hair, ruffled her skimpy costume and made her shiver. She missed San Francisco, she missed her old life, and for the first time in months, the urge to pack up and go home was stronger than ever.

She thought about her ballet days, the elegant venues she'd danced in, women in sparkling jewels, men who appreciated the art rather than the bodies involved. The applause and the praise, the red roses thrown at her feet, the orchestra members in the pit. She may have lost that part of her life but Vivian's words in the dressing room reminded her that it didn't have to be over. *You could be an instructor, open up your own ballet school.*

"Ellie?" She turned to see Luke standing at the back door with a concerned look on his face. "Why are you crying?"

Startled, she lifted her hand to her face and felt the moisture there. When had she started crying?

"I..." Her throat tightened. "I don't know."

Before she could blink Luke was beside her. He drew her into his arms and held her against his chest, his embrace filling her body with warmth. "I can't stand to see you cry," he murmured, pressing his face against the top of her head.

Her tears soaked through the cotton of his shirt and yet she still wasn't quite sure why she was crying in the first place. Maybe it was because her entire world had crumbled beneath her again, slid away like grains of sand through her fingers. She didn't have a reason to be in this town anymore. No job, no Vivian to depend on. And it made her feel so damn helpless.

As a small sob slipped out of her mouth, Luke ran his hands over her trembling shoulders and threaded his fingers through her hair. Then he planted a feather-light kiss on her forehead and whispered, "Come on, baby, let me take you home."

"Here, I hope I made it the way you like it." Luke handed her a steaming mug of tea before joining her on the sofa.

She thanked him and accepted the cup, then moved into a cross-legged position and took a long sip. The warm liquid slid down her throat and soothed her insides. When they'd returned to the bungalow she'd changed into a pair of comfortable sweatpants, a faded old T-shirt and thick wool socks, but for some reason she still felt cold.

"Why do you think Viv lied to me about Josh?" she asked softly.

A pained look entered Luke's gray eyes as he shifted in his seat. "Honestly? I think there's something going on between the two of them."

She nearly dropped her mug. "Are you serious?"

Luke shrugged. "It's just a feeling."

Ellie set down her cup, leaned back and laced her fingers together. Josh and Vivian? No. That didn't make any sense. Though she loved them both deeply, she couldn't imagine them as a couple. Josh was uptight and rigid, while Vivian was the most adventurous free spirit Ellie had ever met. What did they even have in common? And if there was something between them, why hadn't Vivian told her?

As if reading her thoughts, Luke's low voice broke through the silence. "Vivian cares about you. She never meant to hurt you or lie to you."

"Well, she did." She swallowed back the lump of pain clogging her throat. "I can't believe she fired me."

"Ellie, about that..." His tone faltered. "Vivian's not the only one to blame for that."

She snapped to attention. "What do you mean?"

"I kind of asked her to do it."

"You!" Disbelief filled her face before dissolving into triumph. "I knew it. Viv denied it but deep down I knew she wouldn't have done it unless someone else talked her into it."

With a low-pitched growl she shot to her feet, fighting the ridiculous urge to kick him in the shin.

"I don't appreciate your meddling." She crossed her arms over her chest and sent a glare in his direction. "Or the way you

163

went behind my back."

"Oh really?" he shot back. "Well, look who's turned into a hypocrite."

She narrowed her eyes. "What's that supposed to mean?"

"It means, Elenore, the next time you want to make me jealous by pretending to have a date, make sure the eligible bachelor isn't gay."

Her jaw dropped. What...how...how had he known? The little smirk on his face told her he'd figured out all about Miguel, though for the life of her she didn't know how he'd done it. Miguel had been more than convincing. Hadn't he?

She stared at Luke, suddenly reminded of the way he'd held her in the alley, how she'd felt cradled in his strong arms. And he'd called her *Baby*, she remembered that too. But what did it mean? What did she want it to mean?

She searched his smoky gray eyes, wondering what he was feeling. Had he called her that just to comfort her? Or was there more to it?

Overwhelmed by the possibilities, she stepped toward him. Swept her gaze over his face, the dark stubble on his powerful jaw, the tiny lines around his mouth. A shiver danced through her body as she watched him. He met her eyes, dropped his gaze to her lips, then back up. Neither of them spoke. They didn't have to. Since the second she'd admitted her attraction to him back in her dressing room she'd known how this night would end.

With a burst of confidence, she reached for his hand and gently pulled him to his feet. She held her breath, waiting, then released it when he ran his thumb along her jaw line. "I thought you said all deals are off the table," he murmured.

"This isn't a deal or a game to me anymore," she whispered. "And I need to know it's not that way for you either."

Chapter Eleven

"God help me, but it isn't." Luke's rough voice made her tingle. So did the way he continued stroking her face. "I'm sick of games."

"Me too."

He cupped her chin with his warm hands and she almost melted into a puddle on the floor. "I want you." He dipped his head and ran his lips over the curve of her neck, planting wet kisses along her fevered skin. "Since the second I saw you that first night at the club. I've tried to fight it."

She shivered as he moved his mouth to her ear and kissed it. "Are you still fighting?"

He slid his hands to her waist and pulled her to him. Made sure she could feel the hard ridge of his erection against her belly.

"Does it feel like I am?" he murmured before closing his mouth over hers.

He kissed her, a long thrilling kiss that sent waves of rapture cascading down her body. His mouth was slow and gentle. So unlike the hungry, urgent kisses he'd given her last night. She lost herself in the taste of him, in his spicy, intoxicating scent. They could have been standing there for hours. Or days. Or months. Time ceased to exist as Luke's tongue explored her mouth and his hands her body. When he lifted her in his arms, she wrapped her legs around him in response, and allowed him to carry her into her bedroom.

He dropped her on the bed then stood at the foot of it. A sliver of moonlight floated through the open slit of the window curtains, lighting up Luke's face and making the hunger in his eyes glimmer.

"Last time we were in this position I never took the time to find out what makes you feel good. To drive you wild."

"Trust me, you drove me wild."

"Maybe so, but tonight I'm taking my time." He unzipped his jeans. "If you don't mind, that is."

"I don't mind."

The sight of him in his snug boxer-briefs unleashed ripples of anticipation in her stomach. His erection made an impressive tent in the cotton but he seemed completely unabashed by it. Moving closer, he took off his shirt, and then settled on the edge of the bed. The mattress sagged under his weight, eliciting more anticipation. She wanted to feel that big powerful body pressing down on her, not the mattress.

Luke didn't say a word as he leaned forward and pulled her T-shirt over her head. He threw it aside, and started working on the front clasp of her bra. The second her breasts popped out of their restraints they were covered again by Luke's hands. He cupped them, his touch more firm than gentle, and started rubbing her nipples with his thumbs.

Shooting her a sexy grin, he asked, "How am I doing? Driving you wild yet?"

"No."

"No?" He lifted his brows. "Not into fondling?"

"Fondling is nice. Your mouth would be better."

He shifted again, this time sliding down so that he lay next to her. There was a spark of challenge in his eyes as he murmured, "You asked for it."

Before she could take a breath he latched his mouth onto one breast, sucking her nipple hard. She gasped, not out of pain but out of the sheer pleasure his skilled pressure provided. She heard him chuckle, the sound thudding against her breast and making her skin burn.

"Better?" He lifted his head and shot her a look of amusement.

"A little."

"A little?" He let out a soft "tsk" before dipping down again to lavish the same attention on her other breast. He was far from gentle, sucking and nipping at her hardened nipples until she cried out with pleasure that bordered on pain, but she wasn't complaining. Arousal drummed through her body, until her thighs grew slick from her own wetness and her hands clawed at the bed sheets.

She bit back a groan when he finally stopped his erotic assault. No, not yet. She didn't want to lose those incredible sensations just yet.

"Don't worry," he teased, obviously catching the disappointment in her eyes. "We're only getting started."

He hooked his thumbs under the waistband of her sweats and pulled them down her hips, taking her panties along for the ride.

"I want to taste every inch of you, Elenore."

His low mutter caused a hot flush to swarm over her skin. "But..." Her voice trailed as he dragged his tongue from her breasts to her stomach and circled her navel.

"But what?" He nipped at her flushed skin, his mouth dangerously close to the sparse triangle of hair between her thighs.

"I need you inside me," she choked out.

"Too bad. I guess you'll have to be patient, won't you?" His husky voice was laced with both satisfaction and amusement. God, he was trying to kill her, wasn't he?

Her eyelids fluttered closed as he kissed her inner thighs then ran his finger over the moisture he'd left there. When she felt the first flick of his tongue against her clit, she gasped again.

The sight of Luke between her legs was probably the sexiest thing she'd ever seen. The feel of his tongue on her clit was even sexier. She gave a throaty little moan that she couldn't believe came from her, then lost herself in the pleasure he was intent on giving her.

"Still feeling impatient?" he teased.

She swallowed back another moan. "A little."

"Does this make it better?" He sucked her gently.

"Yeah," she managed to choke out.

He kissed her wet folds, tonguing her in a way that had her struggling for breath. "What about this?"

"Ah...oh God, uh..."

"Good?"

She managed a nod.

"And this?" He captured her clit with his mouth again and at the same time slid a finger deep inside her.

Her inner muscles instantly tightened over his finger. A shaky breath squeezed out of her lungs as he began a slow torturous rhythm. Licking, pushing his finger deeper, sucking, sliding his finger out. It was almost too much to bear, the pleasure building inside of her, swirling around and just waiting to explode.

"Let go, baby. I want you to come."

Maybe she would have said something else, told him she wanted them to come together, but the moment he pushed another finger inside her she exploded.

Moan after moan slipped from her throat, shudder after shudder racked her body. The room started spinning so she pressed her hands on Luke's head, wanting to steady herself, wanting to hold onto him as the most intense orgasm of her life crashed over her.

Only when she began to tremble did Luke ease the pressure on her clit and lift his dark head. He slid up the bed. Looked at her with eyes narrowed with pure satisfaction.

She blinked, feeling like she'd emerged from a hazy dream and in a raspy voice said, "God, Luke, that was..."

He nuzzled her neck. "That was what?"

"Incredible." She shivered. "But not enough. I need more. I need you."

"Good." His expression was rueful as he glanced down at his crotch. "Because I need you too."

Feeling bold, she skimmed her hand down his chest, brushing over the feathering of hair until she reached his erection. "I see that you do."

He leaned down and kissed her, his tongue swirling and exploring, while she continued her own exploration with her hand. She lost herself in the kiss, groaning when he finally broke it to shuck his boxers.

With a quick peck to her lips he moved his body over hers. She saw the sparkle of desire and anticipation in his eyes as his tip brushed over her opening and a rush of need filled her body. God, she wanted him. Again. Forever.

He gripped her thighs with his palms and spread her legs

wider, and they groaned, simultaneously, as he slid into her. Inch by inch. Until his cock was buried deep in her center.

Her nipples hardened against his chest, and she found herself wet again. Ready to go again. Pressing her hands on his back, she drew lazy circles over his skin with her fingernails and arched her hips, taking him in deeper.

He moved inside her slowly at first, as if he wanted to make every second last but she saw in his pained eyes that he wanted to let go.

"I was going to spend the entire night making up for the last time," he said in a strangled voice.

"Oh, you will. Later." She dropped her hands to his buttocks and squeezed. "Right now I just want to see you lose control."

A small grin lifted the corners of his sexy mouth but it didn't stay there for long. In an instant his features grew taut and he was plunging into her.

"More," she whispered, bucking her hips. "Faster."

He quickened his pace, and thrust his tongue inside her mouth with the same fervor his erection thrust in her warmth. She felt his climax building, knew her own wasn't far behind, and she wrapped her legs around him, wanting to feel his heart thudding against her breasts when they toppled over the edge.

They came together, hard and fast. She cried out his name, and he buried his face in the damp curve of her neck with a ragged groan.

White-hot shards of pleasure shattered before her eyes, sucking all the breath from her body. She held on to Luke's sweat-soaked back as if he were a life preserver and opened her mouth eagerly to let his tongue enter it again.

As the waves of release finally subsided, Luke slowly rolled over and pulled her into his arms. "I can't move my legs," he mumbled.

She pressed her cheek on his chest and enjoyed the erratic beating of his heart against her ear. Raising her head, she looked at him with dazed, sated eyes, opened her mouth, closed it, and then smiled.

Vivian sat motionless in the front seat of her Jeep staring at the darkened house in front of her. She wondered if Josh was asleep. God, she hoped so. She wasn't in the mood to talk to him right now. She was still feeling shell-shocked from Ellie's abrupt dismissal of her, from that hurt and angry look in her friend's eyes when she'd admitted Josh was in town.

Glancing back at the dark windows of her living room, she wondered when she'd become so chicken she couldn't even walk into her own home. She let out a long sigh and glanced at the digital clock on the car stereo. Three-fifteen a.m. Usually she left the club once the girls finished their second performance around midnight, letting the staff close up for the night, but tonight she'd found reasons to stay. All so she wouldn't have to go home and face Josh.

He had to be sleeping by now, which suited her just fine.

Tonight she'd realized what a fool she'd been. No matter how sweet Josh was, no matter how wonderful he made her feel, she was simply too old for him. Three days with him around and she'd become the child she'd accused him of being. Sneaking around with her friend's brother, stashing him in her house, lying about it. She was carrying on like a teenager, for God's sake, and enough was enough.

In a few months she'd turn forty-five and that meant she needed to start acting her age again. Making love to Josh would be so easy, but giving him the relationship he wanted wouldn't. Sooner or later they'd reach a crossroads. He'd want more than she could give and they'd end up going their separate ways. So why prolong the inevitable?

It was time to send him home. With Ellie out of a job, Josh got what he came for. Not all he'd come for but the most important part, anyway.

Turning off the engine, she got out of the Jeep and gently closed the door. The entire neighborhood was silent and the deserted street made her feel oddly wistful. Sometimes she really missed the city, the clutter of cars on the Golden Gate, the chattering of people as they walked past the open windows of her downtown apartment. Had she done the same thing as Ellie? Moved to a place where she didn't belong?

Vivian shrugged away the thought and stepped up the front lawn toward the door. The house was dark and quiet when she entered it. She squinted in the darkness, relieved by the absence of light seeping under Josh's closed door. Looked like there wouldn't be any heavy, emotionally draining talks tonight.

Eager not to wake him, she slid out of her heels and walked barefoot toward the kitchen, where she found the unopened bottle of whiskey in the cabinet under the sink. It had been a gift from one of her dancers but since she normally didn't drink she'd tucked it away for a rainy day.

Or a very late night when only alcohol could drain away the tension in her body.

After pouring herself a glass she soundlessly moved toward the glass patio doors and stepped onto the deck. The moon overhead was full. Didn't that just figure. Full moons always left her feeling restless. She very rarely got a good night's sleep when one of those perfect pale yellow circles filled the sky.

A splashing noise from below made her jump. Riveting her

gaze to the kidney-shaped pool, she bit back a groan as she saw Josh emerge from the dark water. He climbed the steps in the corner of the shallow end, six feet of dripping wet, toned muscle. When he reached the stairs of the deck he stopped in his tracks.

She couldn't unglue her gaze from him, just watched him standing there in the shadows as her throat grew so dry she could barely swallow. He really was magnificent-looking.

"You're still up," she finally uttered, then felt like a complete idiot for stating the obvious.

"I was waiting for you." He ascended the deck stairs, his bare feet leaving wet marks on the cedar. "I thought I'd take a quick dip to pass the time."

The closer he came the faster her heart thumped. His body looked as if it had been sculpted out of marble. Rock-hard and chiseled.

"How did it go with Ellie?" he asked.

"It was awful." Obvious torment washed over her features and when Josh took a step toward her she knew he'd seen it. Before he could pull her into his arms she jolted back.

Uncertainty shone in his dark-blue eyes. "What's wrong?"

What's wrong? There were so many things wrong here she didn't even know where to begin. "I've been doing a lot of thinking," she said simply.

"Why don't I like the sound of that?" He bent to pick up the towel on the patio chair then ran it over his bare chest. "So what have you been thinking about?"

His stab at nonchalance didn't fool her. "That it's time for you to go."

He set his jaw. "I see."

"Look, your sister is furious with me, and I don't blame her.

But I still believe firing her was the right thing to do. I think she'll be coming home any day, which means there's no reason for you to stick around."

"No reason?" he echoed. "What about us? Isn't that reason enough?"

"There is no us. We had a nice dinner, shared a few kisses, but that's all. What did you think, that we'd get married?"

He remained silent.

"The bottom line, Josh, is that I'm too old for you. Not only that but I don't have time to screw around. I have a club to run, and you have a law practice to go back to. We're in different places in our lives. Truth is, we always will be."

"That's bullshit."

"No, it isn't. It's reality. Marriage aside, what about kids? You can't tell me you don't want children."

He chuckled. "You're not that old, sweetheart. Women far older than you are still having babies."

"But I don't want to have any more babies."

"Then we won't have kids."

Frustration seeped into her body and swirled down to her gut. "What's it going to take to make you realize it won't work between us?"

"A hell of a lot more than flimsy excuses."

Her temples started throbbing. Damn it, why did he have to be so stubborn? Why couldn't he just accept it wasn't going to be?

Before she could open her mouth to speak, the sound of the telephone rang out, muffled through the closed patio door. Vivian's frustration instantly transformed into alarm. It was nearly four in the morning. Nobody called her this late unless it was an emergency.

Without another word she spun around and entered the house. The phone was sitting in its cradle and she snatched it up quickly. "Hello?"

"Mom, it's me."

Her alarm deepened. "Tanya, is everything all right?"

"Everything is great!"

To Vivian's relief, excitement poured out of her daughter's voice. "Jeez, sweetie, you had me worried. Do you realize what time it is?"

"I knew you'd be working so I waited until I was sure you were home."

She sighed, wanting to scold her daughter for giving her such a scare but at the same time touched that Tanya had stayed up to the wee hours of the morning to call her. Obviously she had some big news to share. "So what's so urgent you had to lose sleep over?"

"I got into law school!"

A balloon of pride inflated in Vivian's chest, causing her heart to soar. "Oh my God! I thought the letters weren't being sent out for another month."

"They're not. But I got a personal phone call from the head of admissions at..." Tanya paused for effect, "...Harvard Law!"

As Tanya's words sunk in, Vivian resisted the urge to let out a loud shriek of joy. God, she'd worked so hard for this. Scrimping and saving to pay for Tanya's college tuition, pouring over those applications with her for a week straight, and it had all paid off. Her baby girl's dream had come true.

"I can't tell you how happy I am, sweetie." She clung to the phone tightly, wishing Tanya were standing in front of her so she could give her a big hug.

From the corner of her eye Viv saw Josh enter the room,

still clad in swim trunks. For a moment all she could do was shoot him an excited smile, her happiness over her daughter's news taking precedence over everything else. Her smile soon faded at Tanya's next words.

"I think I'm going to give Josh Dawson a call."

The phone shook in her hands. "Oh. Uh, Ellie's brother?"

"Yeah, you remember him, right, Mom? He's a lawyer so I thought I'd arrange to get together with him, you know, get his advice and ask for tips about making it through law school alive."

Vivian swallowed. "That's a great idea, sweetie. I'm sure he'd love to help you."

Tanya giggled. "Even if he doesn't, it'll be worth it if only to see him again. The guy is seriously hot."

A wave of sickness splashed over her like slap to the face. Hearing her daughter call Josh "hot" made her feel like a...like a cradle-robber. What the hell was the matter with her? Josh should be dating her daughter, not her. If she'd doubted it before, she sure as hell didn't doubt it now.

"So anyway," Tanya continued, still sounding as if she was on cloud nine, "I'll let you get to bed. But I'll call you tomorrow morning with all the details, okay?"

"Sounds good, hon."

"I love you, Mom."

"I love you too."

Vivian's eyes were stinging as she hung up the phone. God, she was such a fool. Bottom lip trembling, she turned to Josh and said, "My daughter thinks you're seriously hot."

A look of understanding softened his features. "That doesn't mean anything."

"Yes it does. You should be dating someone your own age.

Someone like my daughter." She let out a breath. "God, imagine what she'd think if I told her about us?"

"Vivian—"

She held up her hand. "This is ridiculous, Joshua." She placed emphasis on his full name, knowing she sounded like his mother and wanting him to see it. "I'm putting a stop to this. Right now."

He tried to speak but she cut him off again. "Whatever was happening between us is over. I want you to leave."

"You don't mean that."

She ignored his rough plea. "Tomorrow morning I want you to go see your sister and explain why you've been lurking around. When you get back you're going to pack up your things and get on the next plane to San Francisco. I'm serious, Josh. You have no reason to stay here. I'm making it clear, right here and right now, that nothing will ever happen between us."

"Luke, are you awake?"

Ellie nudged his bare arm, the only part of his gloriously sexy body not tangled in the bed sheets. He made an unintelligible sound and rolled over, providing her with a very nice view of his bare ass. God, he looked cute when he slept. Gone was the take-charge, I'm-always-in-control bodyguard. His features softened in slumber, making him appear younger. Sweeter.

She bit back a laugh. If he knew she was calling him sweet, he'd have a fit.

Climbing out of the bed, she fumbled around the dark room, looking for her robe. It was nearly four in the morning, but she wasn't tired.

She slipped into her robe and glanced at Luke again, resisting the urge to jump on him and splatter kisses all over his chiseled face. Why had she never known how good sex could be? It amazed her to think about what she'd been missing out on all these years.

Her bare feet tingled, suddenly longing for a pair of ballet slippers. She wanted to dance, wanted to shout out from the rooftops how utterly happy she was.

Leaving the bedroom, she padded down the hall. She paused in front of the living room sliding doors and looked out at the ocean, midnight blue waves rippling under the silver moon. A full moon, she noted. Maybe that explained what had happened tonight. People often credited full moons with eerie events. Not that making love to Luke had been eerie. It had been...right. But unexpected.

Six months ago, the thought of going to bed with Luke would have been preposterous. Inconceivable. Yet it had happened.

Unlatching the door, she slid it open and stepped into the backyard. The sand beneath her feet was soft. And warm. So was the air. Breathing in the salty humid air, she took a step forward, her eyes focused on the water as a thought slipped into her mind.

They hadn't used protection.

She wondered how long it would take before Luke realized it. He hadn't brought it up, but she knew he would.

She absently reached down and stroked her stomach, a motion she'd repeated constantly during the three months she'd been pregnant. Just a tiny bump. She'd lost the baby before it became a protruding bulge.

She'd never realized just how much she'd wanted to be a mother until she'd gotten pregnant. All she'd wanted since she was a kid was to dance, but that had changed once that home-pregnancy test had turned blue. She'd been ready to give up everything for her child. Speed up the wedding. Sacrifice her ballet career, which had just started to take off.

A bitter laugh escaped her throat. Well, she hadn't had to make any sacrifices. She'd lost the child she was carrying. Lost her career. Her fiancé. The future she'd never realized she'd wanted.

"Ellie? Why are you out here?"

But she had Luke. She turned to see him at the door, wearing a pair of boxer-briefs that clung to his lean hips. Bare-chested, with his dark hair tousled from sleep, he was the most appealing sight she'd ever encountered.

Her gaze swept over the rippled chest that moments ago she'd been nestled on, the powerful arms that had embraced her, the talented mouth that had driven her over the edge time and time again. The erection that appeared the second she laid eyes on his groin. Yes, she had Luke. For now, at least.

"I couldn't sleep," she admitted.

He wrapped his arms around her from behind, kissing the top of her head, and she let herself sink into his warmth. Silent, they watched the water lap against the sand and listened to the crash of the waves and sleepy wailing of the gulls.

When he spoke again, what he said didn't surprise her. "I didn't use protection."

"I know." Her voice quiet, she turned and pressed her face against his chest, inhaling the scent of him. "It's okay."

He lifted her head with his hands and forced her to look at him. "You were protected?"

Swallowing the lump in her throat, she said, "Yes."

She expected to see relief in those gray eyes. Maybe even

pleasure. But he remained emotionless. A thousand questions bit at her tongue but she held them at bay. She didn't want to ruin anything. This night had been too wonderful to destroy with after-sex questions. What's going to happen? What does this mean? Where do we go from here?

Tonight they'd all go unanswered.

"The ocean is beautiful at night," he murmured, holding her tighter. "Peaceful."

She rested her cheek against his shoulder. "That's one of the things I like best about living here. God, I love the ocean." She sighed. "My parents did too."

The heat of his hand seeped into her back. "Do you still miss them, Ellie?"

"Every day." She tilted her head to look up at him. "Do you miss your mother?"

His eyes grew cloudy, a swirl of black and gray tinted with pain. "Yes." His Adam's apple bobbed. "It's her birthday next week. The day I dread year after year."

"Dread?" she echoed, confused.

"My dad," he explained in a hoarse voice. "He calls me every year and invites me to spend Mom's birthday with them."

Them? Ellie's confusion deepened but she couldn't find a tactful way to voice her questions. Though he rarely talked about her, Ellie knew Luke's mother had died when he was in college. Since Ellie knew what it was like to lose a parent, she'd never pushed Luke to talk about his mom, but now she had to wonder if the loss had affected the surviving Russell men more than she'd thought.

"He still hasn't accepted the fact that she's dead," Luke said, sparing her from coming up with a way to ask about it. "He acts like she's still alive. He cooks dinner for two every night, for Christ's sake."

"I'm sorry, Luke. I didn't know."

He pinned her down with a harsh look. "Oh no, don't say it like that. I know what you're thinking."

She slipped out of his embrace. "Excuse me?"

"My father isn't crazy, Ellie. I won't send him away."

Shock spilled into her bloodstream. "That's not what I was thinking at all."

"No?" Sarcasm sliced through his tone. "That's what Robin suggested I do. She couldn't stand the fact that I refused to cut him out of my life. Apparently a loony father-in-law put a damper on her plans."

Ellie grabbed for his arm and dug her fingers into his skin, gluing her gaze to his. "Well, I'm not Robin. I would never ask you to cut off your own father."

She dropped his arm and hugged her chest tightly, trying to keep her anger at bay, but the very fact that he'd compared her to his ex made her want to spit nails. Didn't he know her by now? She'd lost both her parents, for God's sake, she'd never advise someone to shun the only family they had left.

"You know what I was thinking when I said I was sorry?" she shot out. "I was thinking how long it's been since I've seen your dad and how I'd like to visit him again."

Luke blinked. "What?"

"You heard me."

"Why would you want to visit him?"

She erased the distance between them and touched his cheek. "Because I remember him being a wonderful man and it breaks my heart knowing he's in pain."

"You'd really want to see him like that?"

"He needs human contact, Luke. The more he's alone the more he'll start to slip away. I don't think you should ever stop seeing him. It's your job to show him he's still got something to live for. Your job to keep him connected to reality."

The side of Luke's mouth lifted in a smile. He drew her into his arms and pressed a kiss to the top of her head. "I'm sorry I compared you to Robin. I know you're nothing like her."

Ellie pressed her face against his collarbone and breathed in the spicy scent of his bare skin. "It's okay."

She felt his warm breath on her hair. "It's just...I feel so bad for him, Ellie. He's just wasting his life away. He won't even let himself mourn the woman he loved."

With a ball of emotion lodged in her throat, she leaned up and pressed her mouth to his in a slow, soft kiss.

"What was that for?" he asked when she pulled back.

Tenderness reflected in his gray eyes, stealing her breath. She tried to speak but all that came out was, "I just...I..."

Love you.

The thought should have shocked her, but it didn't. Instead it filled her with a sense of tranquility. She thought about the first time she'd met him. He'd driven Josh home in his beat-up old Volkswagen, dressed in a denim jacket riddled with holes, his dark hair cut in a sexy, shaggy way that made her heart thump. Maybe she'd fallen in love with him then, that very first day. Or maybe it had happened when he'd held her in his arms tonight like she was a fragile piece of china. She couldn't pinpoint the exact moment but she didn't need to.

All that mattered was the burst of love and tenderness that overflowed in her heart right now.

"Dance with me," she murmured, twining her arms around his neck.

He chuckled. "There's no music."

"Yes there is. You just need to listen."

He slid his hands to her hips as she pressed her cheek to his chest. And they danced, under the moonlight, to the symphony of waves and wind and gulls. After a while, even the sounds of the night seemed to fade away. They were the only people on the beach, in the world, and at that moment, nothing else mattered.

A flood of urgency rushed through her suddenly, as if tonight would be the last night she had with Luke. She kissed him again.

He seemed surprised by her hurried kisses, but he responded quickly, weaving his fingers through her hair and angling her mouth for better access. Their tongues dueled, until he let out a low groan and parted her robe with his hands.

He lowered her onto the sand and dragged his mouth across her breasts, while she stared up at the ink-colored sky and the white moon that overpowered it. Then she closed her eyes and sighed with pleasure as Luke teased her body with his tongue. His mouth hovered between her thighs, and, feeling wanton, she parted her legs and greedily took all that he gave.

Lying there under the vast sky, with the breeze dancing across her exposed body, thrilled her. "I want you inside," she whispered, running her hand through his messy hair and nudging him.

He slid up her body, shucking his boxers, and in an instant he plunged his cock inside her. Utter completion.

Feeling him throbbing inside her, she arched her hips to meet his hurried thrusts. She heard the waves crashing on the shore, as loud and powerful as the wave building inside her. She clung to him, her breaths jerky and erratic, and when the first surge of climax swelled, she cried out his name.

Pleasure like nothing she'd ever experienced, ever dreamed of, filled every nerve ending. It made her shudder and writhe, moan and whimper. Luke leaned down and kissed her, swallowing her cries with his hot mouth, before letting out a cry of his own. She held him as he let go, kissed his face and chest as he jerked inside her. When he collapsed on top of her, his chest slick with sweat, his breath warm against her neck, she held him tighter.

She didn't know how long they lay there, didn't care.

"Ellie, I..." His voice faltered, but the sheer emotion flickering in his eyes, the satisfaction and tenderness, told her all she needed to know.

Chapter Twelve

Luke woke up with a smile and a hard-on. Christ, how was this humanely possible? He'd made love to Ellie nearly half a dozen times during the night, yet his cock still throbbed. He wanted her. Again. And again. And again.

Her warm sleeping body was spooned against his back, and he rolled over so he could look at her. Smiling, he watched the rise and fall of her chest, the way her eyelids fluttered as if she were having an action-packed dream. Was she dreaming of him? He hoped so.

Sliding out of the tangle of sheets, he got up and quietly walked to the bathroom. Then he tiptoed down the hall toward the kitchen and started brewing a pot of coffee for him and tea for Ellie.

Sipping his morning coffee, he entered the living room and rummaged through his jacket pocket for his cell phone. When he flipped it on, he found thirteen messages in his inbox. All from Josh, of course. Yet he had no desire to return a single one.

"Luke?"

He turned to see her in the doorway, wearing an oversized T-shirt. Even with the sleepy expression on her face, the sight of her took his breath away.

Ellie walked toward him, planted a soft kiss on his lips and then pulled back with a smile. "Good morning."

"Morning."

He handed her a cup of tea and her smile widened. "Thanks," she said, looking touched. "Do you want to sit outside?"

With a nod, he followed her through the patio doors and they sat at the table. Sipping her tea, she watched him over the rim of her mug. "I wanted to talk to you about something." Clasping the cup between her fingers, she met his gaze. "I've been thinking of going back to San Francisco." Her expression clouded. "More so now that I don't have a job."

"Josh will be happy," he said ruefully.

"What about you? Does that make you happy?"

"Bringing you home is the reason I came here, remember?"

Her eyes darkened. "I see."

"You see what?"

She dropped her cup on the table, and the dark liquid splashed over the rim and stained the white wicker. Standing up, she shot a cool look in his direction. "Everything. I see everything."

Her icy tone grated his nerves. Damn, when had she become so difficult to read? Before she could march through the back door into the bungalow, he bounded toward her and grabbed her arm. "What the hell is that supposed to mean?"

"It means you succeeded." He was surprised to see hurt flickering in those blue eyes. "You came here to drag me home, and I know you, Luke, you would've done everything to achieve that goal. Even taking me to bed."

Her harsh accusation hung in the humid morning air, causing anger to spiral through him in sharp waves. He couldn't believe the words had even exited her mouth. He hadn't come here to sleep with her. She was insane if she actually believed that.

He wanted to laugh with disbelief. From the second he'd seen her up on that stage, shaking her hips and wiggling her ass, he'd fought against that carnal need pleading with him to take her. Two weeks of living in a constant state of arousal, two weeks of fighting the temptation that was Ellie. And she was accusing him of using sex to pressure her?

"I can't believe you even said that," he snapped, unable to keep the hurt from his voice.

"Isn't it the truth?" she shot back.

"I told you last night that the games were over, and I meant it. I had no ulterior motive in sleeping with you."

"Then why did you? We both know you're not looking for a relationship."

"And what if I am?"

She faltered. "What?"

"Did you ever stop to think that maybe I want to be with you?"

"Do you?"

Their eyes locked and he just stared at her, searching for an answer. Everything about her distracted him. The scent of her hair. The way her T-shirt outlined those small breasts. Her bare legs. He knew that he wanted her, physically, sexually. But did he want to be with her? After the way Robin had turned his life upside down, the answer should've been no. After seeing his father's slow and painful disintegration these last ten years, the answer should've been no.

So why was the word *yes* biting at his tongue?

"Luke?" Her gaze pierced through him and went straight to

his heart, made it squeeze.

"What the hell is going on here?" came an angry male voice.

Simultaneously, both he and Ellie swiveled their heads in time to see Josh appear from the side of the bungalow.

Luke's gaze went from Josh's enraged face, down to his own bare chest and boxers, to Ellie's barely-clad body, then back to Josh.

Oh shit.

Ellie pulled her jeans up to her hips, straightened out the hem of her T-shirt and shot a glance at Luke, who was throwing on clothes like a madman. The bedroom seemed to lose its soft romantic air as they dressed. Not surprising, considering that Josh was pacing her living room at the moment, waiting to pounce on them.

She'd dealt with her brother's overprotective nature and short temper long enough to know that he wasn't happy with what he'd walked in on. Sure, she could lie, tell him that Luke had just stopped by this morning—and decided to shed his clothing for some inexplicable reason—but Josh wasn't stupid.

"We could say nothing happened," she said feebly, more to herself than to Luke.

Zipping up his jeans, he just stared at her. "Have you ever been able to lie to him?"

"No." She sighed. "Look, let me go out there alone. I'll handle this." He opened his mouth to object but she held up her hand. "Please."

With a brisk nod, Luke buttoned his fly and sat down on the edge of the bed, looking oddly nervous.

Watching him rake his fingers through his hair, she wished Josh hadn't chosen to show up at the most inopportune moment. She and Luke had been...getting somewhere. Where, she didn't know, but she suspected he'd been about to say something important. Something that couldn't wait.

But her brother couldn't wait, either. Patience had never been Josh's strong suit.

Straightening her shoulders, she walked into the living room, prepared for a confrontation. When he heard her footsteps, Josh stopped pacing and looked at her.

The sight of him sent a familiar rush of warmth and fondness to her chest. God, she'd missed him. Her gaze swept over his short brown hair, the exact shade as hers, his serious blue eyes. Even the starched white shirt and shiny loafers warmed her heart. This was Josh, her protector, her annoying older brother, the big-shot lawyer who loved a good verbal sparring.

"Ellie..." He stopped, then opened his arms, and in a second she was crushed in his embrace. "I missed you, kiddo."

She hugged him tightly as every pang of homesickness she'd experienced these past two months slipped away. "I missed you too."

He kissed her forehead before pulling back, his eyes trained on hers. "Are you okay?"

"I'm fine."

His features softened for a moment, before hardening to stone. "Where's Russell?"

"In the bedroom."

"Get him out here. Now." Her brother looked livid.

She set her jaw. "No. Not before I say something to you."

Josh let out a sarcastic laugh. "I'm the one with something to say, Elenore. After the way you took off like that, you're in no position to give orders."

Irritation sparked through her. "Sit down, Joshua."

He arched a brow. "I'd rather stand."

"Fine." She drew in a long breath. "I don't want you freaking out on Luke."

Josh crossed his arms over his chest, staring her down. "Why shouldn't I? I asked him to find you and bring you home, not take advantage of you."

She rolled her eyes. "He didn't take advantage of me."

"Did you sleep with him?"

The fact that the question came from her older brother sent a wave of discomfort to her stomach. "That's none of your business."

"Which means yes." Josh scowled. "I'm going to kick his ass for doing this to you."

She rubbed her face in frustration. "Josh—"

"What the hell was he thinking? He was supposed to bring you home, not take you to bed. He was supposed to protect you."

"Luke isn't my bodyguard. He's not responsible for my safety. Neither are you. Oh, and another thing," she continued, enjoying being the one in charge. "I don't appreciate you going behind my back and getting my friends to lie to me."

Josh had the decency to look guilty. "About that... Look, kiddo, Vivian didn't want to lie to you. I practically twisted her arm to keep my being in town a secret."

At Josh's words, Ellie experienced a quick tug of shame. She remembered the cold way she'd dismissed Vivian in the dressing room last night and the shame deepened. She hadn't even given Viv the chance to explain, hadn't been willing to hear her out. What kind of friend did that make her?

"So you decided to show your face, huh?" The sudden sneer

in Josh's voice was so startling it took her a second to realize he wasn't talking to her, but to Luke, who'd just sauntered into the living room.

"I told you to let me handle it," she said to Luke with annoyance.

"I didn't hear any yelling so I was worried he might've killed you."

Josh's eyes were on fire. "Don't even think about making jokes at a time like this."

Luke sighed. "A time like this? Jesus, it's not the fucking Apocalypse."

"You *slept* with my sister!"

Again, Ellie had no interest in discussing her sex life with her brother, so she quickly spoke up. "Josh, quit being an ass. And Luke, don't antagonize him."

"I wasn't being an ass," Josh said defensively.

"I wasn't antagonizing him," Luke grumbled.

Oh brother. And these two accused *her* of being immature.

She raked a hand through her hair and glared at them both. "I know we've got a lot to talk about it, but to be honest, I really don't feel like it right now."

"What the hell is that supposed to mean?" Josh snapped.

"Just what it sounds like. I don't want to talk right now."

"Ellie," Luke started.

"That goes for you too." She let out a frustrated breath, suddenly wishing Vivian were here. Viv was always good at helping her collect her thoughts.

And right now, her thoughts were all over the place. What had Luke been about to say before Josh stormed in? She had her suspicions, but she wished he'd gotten a chance to tell her what was on his mind. And she really wished she could figure out what was on *her* mind, how she felt about everything that happened last night.

But it was impossible to soul search with these two headstrong men around.

Then again, who said she had to stick around and listen to them bicker?

"You know, I think I'll let you two discuss this amongst yourselves." She glanced at her brother. "I need to see Vivian. Will you give me a ride?"

"No. We're not finished here."

Luke voiced his agreement. "Neither are we, Ellie."

"We'll finish everything later," she said breezily, taking a step toward the hallway. "Josh. The ride?"

She saw the irritation flickering in Luke's eyes, but she didn't let herself back down. She couldn't do this right now, not when her emotions were all jumbled up inside her.

Josh, finally realizing that she wasn't giving in and having this confrontation right now, muttered, "Let me get my keys," and then followed her to the front door.

Dropping his sister off at Vivian's place was one of the most difficult things Josh had ever done. It took every ounce of willpower not to storm inside that green and white house, grab Vivian by the shoulders and shake some sense into her, but pride had held him back. Or maybe defeat.

Last night, Vivian had made her feelings clear. It was over. And no matter how badly he wanted to fight her on this, he wasn't the kind of man who begged for a woman's affection. She'd made up her mind, she didn't want to be with him, and heart wrenching as that was, he needed to accept it.

He just wished she could've given him the chance to prove how much he cared about her. Josh had never met another woman like Vivian, a woman who could set his body on fire and at the same time unleash a tender side he never knew he had. If she just got over her silly fears, her unfounded insecurities, she'd see that they made one dynamite couple.

And yet he wasn't sure he blamed her for ending it either. When Tanya had referred to him as hot, it had been awkward to say the least. For one split second Josh had seen where Viv was coming from, how embarrassed it made her feel to be attracted to a man young enough to date her daughter. But that didn't mean he agreed with her point of view one hundred percent. Truth was, she was attracted to him, and the connection between them was foolish to ignore.

Get over it, man.

With a sigh, Josh turned right onto Ellie's street, knowing he had to put Vivian out of his mind and focus on the other issue currently complicating his life. Luke and Ellie.

His hands tightened over the steering wheel as the memory of his best friend and little sister, barely dressed, flashed across his brain. Christ, what was Luke thinking? Why had he decided to add Ellie to his string of casual conquests?

Josh loved Luke like a brother, but that didn't mean he condoned the guy's behavior. Ever since Luke's relationship with Robin had fizzled, he'd been living it up as a bachelor, moving from one woman to the next, never sticking around long enough for a second date. Well, Josh wouldn't let his friend take advantage of Ellie. His sister was the most important person in his life and damn it, she'd been hurt enough the past six months. Josh wouldn't let her get hurt again.

Stiffening his shoulders, he parked his rental behind

Luke's SUV and entered the bungalow. "Get your ass out here, Russell," he called the second he stepped into the living room.

A moment later, Luke walked out of the kitchen. "I take it it's time for round two?"

"You're lucky Ellie decided to leave. You wouldn't have wanted her around to see me kicking your ass." Even to his own ears the threat sounded hollow.

Luke rolled his eyes and met Josh's icy stare, unfazed. "You seriously want to pick a fight with a bodyguard? Don't you remember the last time we got in a fistfight? As I recall, someone's ass did get kicked and it certainly wasn't mine."

"I was fifteen, I've picked up a few moves since then." He stared his friend down then broke out in a reluctant grin. They both knew Luke was right. Though a fight between them would probably be close, Josh suspected Luke would come out the winner. He always had in the past.

After a brief moment, his grin faded into a scowl. "What the hell are you thinking, man? Why Ellie?"

Luke seemed confused. "What do you mean?"

"Look, I'm not knocking your lifestyle, but you don't have a good track record with relationships. You can have any woman you want, any night you want. Why couldn't you leave Ellie alone?"

"It's not like that."

Josh shot him a knowing look. "No? As I recall, after you left Robin, you were dead set on never getting involved again. What the hell changed?"

Luke opened his mouth to reply, and then clamped it shut. Josh's question hung in the air, making him hesitate. What had changed? What was he doing with Ellie? What did he want from her?

He rubbed his forehead, momentarily confused. He wanted...well, damn, he wanted a lot of things. He wanted to make love to her again. To dance with her the way they had last night. To hold her in his arms every night until they fell asleep. To spend each and every day making her smile that sassy smile of hers.

He suddenly cursed out loud.

"Great answer," Josh said sarcastically. "Makes me real happy I asked you to help me with Ellie."

Luke let out a frustrated breath. "Damn it, man, cut the sarcasm."

"Not until you tell me why on earth you got involved with my little sister."

With a strangled groan, he said the first thing that came to mind. "Because I love her."

If he hadn't been so shocked by his own revelation, he might have laughed at the sight of Josh's dropped jaw. It took a lot to catch Josh Dawson off-guard.

"You love her?"

He turned his head and focused his gaze through the open patio door to that spot on the sand they'd laid on last night. The image of Ellie's naked body and sexy grins flashed through his head, and his pulse quickened. She always did that to him, made his heartbeat race like this.

He could've denied it. Said that he'd uttered the words in haste but really didn't mean them. But damn, deep down he knew he'd meant those three little words. Somehow, between their bickering and their games, between those gentle kisses and mind-blowing sex, he'd fallen in love with her.

"Yes. I do. I'm in love with her, Josh."

His friend exhaled deeply. "Have you told her?"

"No."

"Does she love you?"

He swallowed. "I don't know."

"She does, you know." Josh's shoulders sagged. "I think she's always loved you."

Luke couldn't explain the rush of pleasure that shot through him. He remembered Ellie's confession that she'd wanted him for fifteen years, and cursed himself for being so blind. For not realizing his own feelings sooner.

"She told me why she ran off." He didn't mean to change the subject, but the words slipped out before he could stop them. Thinking about Ellie in the Dancehall reminded him of her other confession. "When she broke her foot...she can't dance ballet again, man."

"What?" Surprise lined Josh's eyes.

"Her career is over. That's why she took off, that's why she's working in Vivian Kendrick's club. It's the only connection she has to her old life, to dancing."

"Why the hell didn't she tell me?"

"I think it was too much for her to handle. That's why she needed to get away."

As silence fell over the room, Luke suddenly needed to sit down. His mind was swimming with questions, the main one being—what did he do now? How did he deal with the knowledge that he'd fallen for Ellie?

He sank onto the couch and rubbed his forehead. A second later Josh joined him, looking equally distressed. Shooting his friend a sideways glance, Luke asked, "Still want to kick my ass?"

Josh smiled faintly. "Naah. But I would like you to promise me something."

"Yeah, what's that?"

"Don't ever hurt my sister, Luke. If you really do love her, I'll give you my blessing. But I need to trust that you won't screw around with her feelings. Either you're there for her for the long haul, or you're not there at all."

"I'm there for the long haul." It shocked him that he actually meant it.

Josh nodded, looking pleased. Then he gave a bitter laugh. "Well, at least one of us got the girl this time."

Luke cocked his head. "You mean, you and Vivian...?"

"Why doesn't it surprise me you figured out there was something between us?" Josh set his mouth in a grim line. "*Was* being the operative word. Vivian ended things last night."

"I'm sorry, man."

"Yeah, so am I." Josh chuckled. "She thinks she's too old for me."

Luke returned the chuckle. "And in one week you couldn't convince her what an old geezer you are? Christ, Josh, you were wearing business suits at the age of eighteen. Oh, and who could forget all those antacids you popped in college while most kids your age lived on a diet of beer?"

A rueful smile lifted Josh's mouth. "I guess Viv couldn't see it. It also didn't help that her daughter called last night and raved about how hot I am." He paused. "That phone call was the final straw for Viv. She thinks Tanya would be horrified if she knew her mother was dating me."

Luke drew his brows together in a frown. "Have you thought about getting in touch with Tanya yourself?"

"Man, you sound like Viv. I don't want to date her daughter, for fuck's sake!"

Luke held up his hand. "Relax, that's not what I meant. I'm

197

just wondering if maybe you can ask Tanya to talk to her. Tanya's a sweet girl, and she adores her mother." He offered a small shrug. "I think she'd just want Vivian to be happy."

A look of uncertainty spread across Josh's face. "You think she'd be okay with me dating her mother?"

"You won't know unless you call her."

Luke saw the wheels turning in his friend's head and when Josh shot to his feet a second later he looked like a new man. "You're right," he announced. "It's definitely worth a shot." He slapped his hands together. "Okay, I need to get a few things from the car. I think Alice jotted down Tanya's number on one of my papers."

With a determined expression Josh strode to the front door but stopped before turning the knob. "I'm really glad about you and Ellie, man," he said over his shoulder. "But remember that promise you made, okay? You need to take care of her. She's so fragile, especially after losing the baby, and, well, she needs to know she can count on you to be there for her."

Josh flew out the door before Luke had a chance to reply or even comprehend what he just heard.

Losing the baby?

Chapter Thirteen

Ellie found Vivian in the backyard, sitting on the concrete deck surrounding the swimming pool. Viv's bare feet dangled over the edge, making absent circles in the water. As Ellie stepped closer a pang of guilt tugged at her stomach. If someone ever wanted to know what the word dejected meant, all they had to do was look at Vivian right now.

"Viv?" she said cautiously, stepping onto the deck.

A look of relief flooded the older blonde's features as she caught sight of her. "Hey! I'm so glad you came by."

"Josh just dropped me off."

"So he finally decided to step out of the shadows and face you."

"Yeah." Ellie lowered herself on the concrete and sat next to Vivian. After a moment, she kicked off her flip-flops and dipped her bare feet into the water.

She tilted her head to look up at the clear blue sky, and then glanced around Vivian's enclosed backyard. Viv was an avid gardener, she'd spent a lot of time planting all the colorful flowers on the perimeter of the yard, and there was something about being surrounded by flowers that soothed Ellie's nerves.

"I'm sorry I lied to you," Vivian said softly.

"Josh put you in an awkward position, I get that now." Ellie wiggled her toes in the cold water. "And Luke confessed he was the one who convinced you to fire me, so you don't need to cover his ass anymore."

"I still think I did the right thing," Viv answered without hesitation. "You don't belong here, honey."

"I think you're right." She breathed in the sweet scent of the flowers. "Why didn't you tell me you had a thing for Josh?"

Vivian gave an uncomfortable laugh. "I guess I didn't want to admit it to myself, let alone share the embarrassment with someone else."

"Embarrassment? What do you mean?"

"I'm forty-four years old, Ellie. I have no business dating a guy Josh's age."

Ellie wrinkled her forehead. "Viv, you have the right to go out with anyone you choose. If you have feelings for Josh, you can't let his age stop you from exploring them."

"You're honestly telling me you'd want your brother to be with me?"

"Why not?" Ellie shrugged and offered a tiny smile. "You might even be good for him. Josh is so uptight, so determined to take care of everyone. I don't think he even knows the meaning of the word relax. You, on the other hand, have mastered it."

Vivian chuckled. "So you want me to loosen him up?"

"Well, God knows he needs it."

Vivian was quiet for a moment, and then she let out a sigh that sounded heavy to Ellie's ears. "Someone else will have to do it then. I'm not the woman for the job, honey."

"Why don't you give it a chance? You might find out you are that woman."

Vivian shook her head. "After last night I'm more than certain Josh needs to be with someone else."

Ellie opened her mouth to object but she never got the chance as Viv swiftly changed the subject to ask, "What about you and Luke? Who won the game of seduction?"

"Me? Him? Both of us? Who knows."

Vivian nodded knowingly. "You slept with him."

"Yes."

"And?"

"And what?"

"Will there be a future for the two of you?"

Ellie lifted her head and let the warm breeze caress her face, remembering what Luke had said before Josh stormed in. *Did you ever think maybe I wanted to be with you?*

Biting her lip, she turned to her friend. "I don't know. I'm too messed up to think about having a relationship with Luke. Or anyone, for that matter."

"Then clean up your internal mess."

"How?"

"Well, first of all, you can stop thinking your life is over just because you can't dance. Like I said before, teaching is always an option."

"I know." She sighed. "I just can't imagine not dancing. For so long, ballet was my entire life. And then, when I got pregnant, the baby became my entire life. Now..." Her voice drifted. "I don't even know who I am anymore. I can't be a dancer, I'll never be able to give birth to my own child, so who can I be?"

"You can be Ellie." Vivian smiled. "You can be a teacher, a wife, a mother to a child who might not be biologically yours but who you'll love just as much. You can be anything you want, hon."

"I can't enter a relationship until I figure it out, Viv. What if Luke doesn't get that?"

"Then he's an ass."

Ellie grinned. "Takes one to know one."

"What's that supposed to mean?"

"It means you should stop being so insecure and give Josh a chance."

"I'll think about it," Vivian said noncommittally.

"Ah, so now you're an ass *and* a liar."

As Ellie approached the edge of her driveway she was suddenly glad she'd decided to walk the twenty minutes across town instead of calling a cab or Josh to pick her up. She'd spent the time seriously thinking about what she wanted to say to Luke, and as she hurried up the front walk she knew it was time to tell him the truth.

The black SUV in the driveway told her Luke was still there, but fortunately Josh's rental car was gone.

When she entered the house, she found Luke in the living room, sitting on the couch and absently flipping through a *Sports Illustrated* magazine. He lifted his head when he heard her come in. "Welcome back."

She glanced around the room. "Where's Josh?"

"He had some errands to take care of."

"Did you two fight?"

"I got a nice verbal beating. But after I made Josh understand the situation, he gracefully gave me his blessing and left. He said to kiss you goodbye, by the way."

Josh had given him his blessing? Blessing for what?

Fiddling with the hem of her T-shirt, she dropped into the nearby recliner and bit her lip. "What exactly did Josh bless?"

"Us."

She ignored the way her heart skipped a beat. "Us?"

Getting up, he languidly strolled toward her. "I told Josh I love you."

Despite the fact that she was sitting down, she nearly keeled over. "What?"

He stroked her palm with his fingers. "You heard me. I told him I love you. And it's the truth." He leaned down and kissed her hand. "I'll be honest, Elenore. You drive me crazy. Sometimes you make me want to tear my own hair out."

"Thank you?"

He chuckled. "But in spite of that, I love you."

"I can't believe you're saying this. I don't know what..." Her voice trailed off.

"C'mere," he grumbled, pulling her into his arms.

She molded against him, savoring the feel of his strong embrace and the soft kisses he planted on her lips. Closing her eyes, she tried to lose herself in his tender touch. He gently pushed her onto her back, trailing his mouth down her neck, lifting her shirt so that he could kiss her stomach.

"Why didn't you tell me about the baby?"

His question sent a jolt of shock thundering through her, and she sat up abruptly, pushing his hand away. "What?"

He reached out again and touched her cheek. "Josh told me about the miscarriage."

"I..." Unable to speak, she stumbled backwards, trying to place some distance between them.

"If it hurts to talk about it, you don't have to. I was just surprised, that's all. I never knew you were pregnant."

"Well, I was," she snapped.

He dropped his hand. "I'm sorry. I shouldn't have brought it up."

Seeing the hurt flickering in his eyes, her face softened. "No. I'm sorry. I didn't mean to snap at you." She drew a long breath. "It's just really painful talking about it."

"I understand." He paused, looking hesitant. "You'll have another child someday, Ellie. And you'll be a wonderful mother."

She nearly choked on her bitterness. "Luke…"

"No, let me say this." He swallowed. "I know I can be a jerk, stubborn at times, maybe a little overbearing. But I promise you, I'm going to spend the rest of my life making you happy. I want us to make a life together. A family. I want to give you a child. I know it won't make up for the one you lost, but…"

"Luke…stop." She swallowed hard, trying not to look at his earnest eyes. "I don't think we should be talking about this right now."

"Why the hell not?"

"Because I'm not ready for it. I can't make any commitments right now."

Again he said, "Why the hell not?"

"Because I'm too confused."

"About me? You think I don't mean what I'm saying?"

"I know you mean it." She drew in a long breath. "This has nothing to do with whether or not you mean it. It has to do with me." She shook her head, suddenly feeling frustrated. "Dancing was my entire life, and now I can't do it anymore. And the accident…I lost more than my baby, Luke. I had a hysterectomy."

He faltered. "You did?"

She nodded, and the sadness that creased Luke's strong features was like a knife twisting in her heart. "I can't have kids. I can't dance. I can't think about moving on with my life without reliving all that pain, Luke."

"I can help you through it."

"You can't. It's something I need to do on my own. I thought coming here, running away from everything, was the answer, but it's not." She sighed. "You and Josh are right. I need to go home and figure out what the hell I'm going to do now that my career is shot to hell."

"Why do you need to figure it out alone?" he asked, looking frustrated.

"Because I don't want to burden you with my problems. Sleeping with you is one thing, but I'm not about to drag you into the process of putting my life back together."

"So what, you think you're protecting me by sparing me from your problems?"

She bit her lip. "Well...yeah."

A short silence fell over the room, and then Luke did something she wasn't expecting, not in the least.

He burst out laughing.

A light rain began to drizzle as Josh headed for the entrance of the Dancehall. Shrugging raindrops off his jacket, he entered the club and wasn't surprised to find it empty. It was three in the afternoon, after all. But Josh hadn't come here for a drink. With a determined lift of his shoulders he made a beeline for the counter.

Vivian had her back turned to him and he took a second to admire the way her long blonde hair fell over her shoulder blades. He loved her hair. Loved the way it felt between his fingers. Hell, he loved everything about her.

"Can I help you?" the man behind the counter asked, cocking his head toward Josh.

Vivian turned around instantly, her eyes widening at the sight of him

"Hi, sweetheart," he said smoothly.

Her eyes grew wider and she shot a quick glance to her bartender, who discreetly moved to the end of the bar. "What are you doing here?" she asked, sliding off her stool. "I thought you'd be—"

"Gone?" he finished. His confidence grew. "Sorry to disappoint you."

She just stood there, looking sexy as hell in a pair of snug jeans and a pink T-shirt that stretched over her breasts. Trying to keep his gaze on her face and not that spectacular body, Josh removed his jacket and tossed it on a nearby chair. Then he moved closer, pleased to see the swell of Viv's chest as she inhaled a sharp breath.

"Where's the phone?" he asked.

The startled look on her face made him bite back a laugh. "The phone? Do you need to make a call?"

"Nope." He grinned. "But you do."

"What?"

"Your daughter is expecting your call, Vivian. I suggest you don't keep her waiting."

The confusion in her eyes gave way to alarm. "Tanya? Is she okay?"

"She's pretty upset, actually." He offered a casual shrug. "I just got off the phone with her."

"Oh God, is this about her scholarship?" Without waiting for a reply, Vivian swiveled around and bent over the counter. She turned with a cordless phone in her hands. "Is she at home?" Vivian asked urgently.

"Yep."

Vivian stared at Josh, wondering what the hell was going on. She wasn't sure she liked that strange little grin on his face, and she sure as hell didn't like his out-of-the-blue phone call with her daughter. With shaky fingers, she dialed Tanya's number and waited.

"Hello?"

"Hi, honey, it's me. Is everything all right?"

"No, actually it's not." Tanya paused. "Why didn't you tell me about you and Josh Dawson?"

Viv stared at Josh with daggers in her eyes, then managed a steady voice as she replied, "I...didn't want to upset you."

"Well, guess what, Mom, I'm upset."

A snake of guilt slithered up her chest, making it hard to take a breath. "I'm sorry, honey, I—"

"How could you possibly think you're too old for him?"

Vivian froze. "What?"

"You heard me. Josh called and told me you'd broken things off because you think you're too old. Because you think I'd be embarrassed to see you two together."

She looked at Josh again, torn between slapping him for going behind her back and speaking to her daughter, and applauding him for taking control of the situation. "I thought..."

"You thought wrong," Tanya announced. She sounded seriously annoyed. "I want you to give him a chance, Mom."

"Did he put you up to this?" She glanced at Josh, her eyes narrowed in suspicion, but he simply offered her a careless shrug.

"No, he didn't." Tanya's tone was firm. "You deserve to be happy, Mom. God knows you worked hard enough all your life to earn that. And if Josh makes you happy, you should see where things go. I'll be furious with you if you don't."

A smiled warmed Vivian's lips. She'd said those same words to her daughter—*I'll be furious with you if you don't*—when Tanya had hesitated about applying for law school, and she got an odd sense of pride hearing those same words being repeated back to her. She'd underestimated her own kid. She'd thought Tanya would be horrified by the way she'd been carrying on with Josh, and Vivian had to wonder if maybe she'd been using what she believed would be her daughter's reaction to mask her own insecurities.

God, she felt immature.

Into the phone, she said, "You really wouldn't think I'm..."

"You're what?" her daughter cut in. "A wonderful, beautiful woman dating a man who obviously adores her? Come on, Mom, I thought you knew me better than that. I only want the best for you."

"You're really an amazing young woman, you know that, Tanya Rose Kendrick?"

"I had a pretty good role model." Tanya's sigh rang out from the other end of the line. "Now don't screw this up, Mother. Like I said, Josh is a hottie. Not only that, but he's smart, kind and totally into you."

When Vivian glanced at Josh again she found herself looking at him in a new light. "I love you, honey," she said into the receiver.

"I love you too. Now stop acting like a child and tell the guy how you feel."

Vivian choked back a laugh as she hung up the phone. Her twenty-four-year-old daughter calling her a child? Well, that was new.

"So?" Josh said. He crossed his arms over his rain-soaked T-shirt, looking expectant.

"She told me not to screw this up."

"She's right."

He stepped closer, planted both hands on her hips and thrust his body against hers. From the end of the counter, Joey the bartender coughed and shuffled away toward the back room. Alone with Josh, Vivian searched his cobalt-blue eyes and asked, "You seriously want to pursue this?"

"Yes."

She swallowed. "I don't know if I'll go back to San Francisco, Josh."

"Then we'll just have to do it long-distance." He grinned. "I hear phone sex is wild."

"And if it doesn't work out?"

"Then it doesn't work out. At least give us a chance." He tightened his grip on her waist and lowered his head so that his lips were inches from hers. "Will you give us a chance, Vivian?"

Her chest ached, but this time it had nothing to do with fear or guilt or shame. It had everything to do with pure and simple joy. "My daughter will kill me if I say no."

"Then you better say yes."

She laughed again. "Okay."

"Okay what?"

"I'll give us a chance."

"Now that's more like it." With the grin never leaving his

handsome face he dipped his head and kissed her until her knees turned to jelly and her limbs turned to liquid.

Until she felt younger and happier than she had in her entire life.

Luke couldn't stop the laughter booming out of his chest. He stared at Ellie, wondering how she could possibly think she was protecting him by breaking things off. He didn't need her protection. He was the bodyguard here. He should be protecting *her*. Taking care of her. So why wasn't she giving him the chance to do that?

"What exactly are you scared of, Ellie?" he asked quietly. "Why did you run off after the car accident?"

She looked caught off-guard. "I just told you why."

"Because you had to leave the ballet company?"

She nodded.

"And because you can't have children?"

She nodded again.

"Why is that the end of the world?"

Her nostrils flared. "It's the end of *my* world, Luke. What will I do if I can't dance?"

He shrugged. "Teach? Go back to college? You've got options, Ellie."

"And I bet you're going to tell me I have options about the child issue too, right? Adoption. Surrogacy." She gave a bitter smile. "Yeah, I know about those options. So did Scott, yet that didn't stop him from dumping me, or telling me that I was damaged because I couldn't give him a family."

"Well, Scott's an idiot. You're not damaged," he said,

fighting back anger that she could even believe such a thing.

"So why do I feel so inadequate?" Her voice sounded forlorn.

"Because you've been trying to deal with all of it on your own these past six months. If you'd actually let someone in, allowed someone to help you, they would've told you that you are the farthest thing from inadequate."

She bit her lip again. "You think so?"

"I know so. You'll never be inadequate, baby," he said softly. He moved closer, lifted one hand to her mouth and brushed his fingers over her lips. "In fact, you're so much woman, sometimes I don't think I can handle you."

She blinked. "Really?"

"Really." He reached for her hand and squeezed it. Her fingers felt cold so he rubbed them between his.

"But you said wanted to be a father."

He sighed. "I do. And if you want, we can have a child, Ellie." She opened her mouth but he cut her off. "Biology is overrated, anyway."

The tears in her eyes made his heart ache. "You'd be okay with that?"

He stared at her in disbelief for a moment, then dipped his head and crushed his mouth over hers, kissing her deeply. When he pulled back, he said, "Ellie, I love you. I want to be with you. I don't care if we adopt ten kids or zero kids. I'm happy as long as I'm with you." He took a breath. "And now that I know what's gotten you so damn scared, there's nothing stopping us from being together. Except you." He met her eyes. "Do you love me, Elenore?"

"You know I do."

Her entire chest filled with warmth at her earnest words.

"Then say it."

She lifted her hand and swept it over his jaw. "I love you," she whispered.

He grinned. "Louder."

"I love you, Lucas."

"Good." He dipped his head and planted a light kiss on her lips. "Now let's go home."

About the Author

To learn more about Elle please visit www.ellekennedy.com. Send an email to elle@ellekennedy.com or visit her blog, the Sizzling Pens, at http://sizzlingpens.blogspot.com.

On the night the Cereus blooms, temptation paints a picture impossible to resist.

Night of the Cereus
© 2008 Anya Delvay

Artist's model Melanie Fletcher likes to keep life simple, and painter Marcus Alejandro practically oozes complications. And sex appeal.

Posing for him, surrounded by the seductive scent of the night-blooming Cereus, Melanie's self-imposed rules of a lifetime are slowly being undermined. She begins to wonder— would it really hurt to give in to her lust, just this once?

Initially drawn to the dichotomy between Melanie's reserved exterior and hidden passion, Marcus soon discovers the more he gets from her, the more he wants. Her delicious body isn't enough. He needs to know her intimately, both inside and out, but getting her to trust him is harder than he ever imagined.

How much can he ask for before she walks away?

Available now in ebook from Samhain Publishing.

Winning the lottery changes her life forever…
in more ways than one.

Fortune's Deception
© 2008 Karen Erickson
Book 1 of the Fortune series.

One minute Brittney Jones is living paycheck to paycheck, and the next she and three friends win a record-breaking lottery jackpot. Sure, she's spent some money on herself—after her rough childhood, she figures she deserves a few indulgences, big and small.

To financial advisor Charlie Manning, his client Brittney is a shallow beauty out to spend all of her money. He thinks she should rein it in. She thinks he should loosen up, and resolves to help him do just that—in a very naughty way.

The passion between them burns hot and fast, and Charlie comes to realize Brittney's heart is as big as her newly fattened bank account. She's not only smart, but beautiful and sexy. And he can't resist her.

Still, Charlie is aware that Brittney's keeping secrets from him. If only she would trust him enough to tell the truth!

Available now in ebook from Samhain Publishing.

GREAT CHEAP FUN

Discover eBooks!

THE FASTEST WAY TO GET THE HOTTEST NAMES

Get your favorite authors on your favorite reader, long before they're out in print! Ebooks from Samhain go wherever you go, and work with whatever you carry—Palm, PDF, Mobi, and more.

Samhain
publishing
Ltd

WWW.SAMHAINPUBLISHING.COM